Finding the Way Home

When love doesn't follow the rules,
but follows the soul

Rona Schweitz

ISBN:

978-1-941883-21-1   Paperback
978-1-941883-22-8   Ebook

Acknowledgements

To the Supreme, who continues to be the Source of all wisdom and the One to guide my every thought and action.

To Mohini Didi for her quiet yet powerful spiritual presence and her vision that always inspires me to do better and to be better.

To the whole Brahma Kumaris family for their immense enthusiasm, courage, and encouragement and their invaluable spiritual companionship.

To Diana Grotte for her constant constructive feedback and her insistent encouragement. Without her this book would not have come into being.

To Wenda Schweitz for being the best mother and a sweet friend.

To Anjali Grover and Guus Pengel for their valuable feedback and encouragement.

To Ronnie Lacey for her invaluable feedback and editing. And to many others who have encouraged, advised, and guided.

Author's Note

This is a work of fiction. The characters and events are products of the author's imagination, though the inner experiences they portray are inspired by the author's own reflections and encounters with meditation. Any resemblance to actual people, living or departed, or to real events, is purely coincidental, except for the Meditation Center at 306 Fifth Avenue, 2nd Floor, Manhattan, New York, which exists in reality.

Table of Contents

To BapDada, for Your endless wisdom
and Your ongoing guidance.

And to all who, consciously or
subconsciously, aim for a life of greater
depth and meaning, this is for you.

CHAPTER 1

The Surprise

Julia's mind was flooded with silence. A peace so profound enveloped her, like the gentle embrace of a long-lost and dearly loved friend. A tranquility, normally elusive yet now almost palpable, flowed through her being, taking her beyond the chatter and noise of her present-day sometimes chaotic existence.

She felt so light, as if not limited to the confines of the physical world. Refined feelings that felt ancient yet familiar were stirred within her, whispering of a time when feeling safe, joyful, and loved were natural.

Time seemed to lose its grip on her as she was immersed in an almost other-worldly stillness, until the mundane sound of a ticking clock shattered the silence, pulling her back to the present moment.

Nicolas, her boyfriend, had arranged a surprise for her birthday, a lecture on 'Habits of Happiness' at the Meditation Center. A gesture both unexpected and puzzling given her general skepticism towards anything to do with meditation and spirituality.

Despite her reservations, Julia found herself drawn to the lecture, held in a spacious room with warm-colored paintings that had a soothing vibe. The people were friendly with welcoming smiles. Though Nicolas was late, due to an emergency at the hospital where he works as a young cardiologist, Julia decided to stay and wait for him while attending the lecture. Though intrigued by the promise of some insights into the nature of happiness, she kept looking at the door, hoping to see Nic come in.

Amidst the many faces, the eyes of the lecturer, Alexandra Clover, captivated her. She was tall and graceful, her thick dark hair woven into a long plait that rested on her back. The loose white clothes she wore seemed to carry the very calm she spoke of. In her presence there was something timeless and quietly powerful. In her eyes, Julia sensed a depth of understanding and an extraordinary benevolence.

Despite her initial reluctance, Julia's interest was aroused, and she even found herself taking some notes on her phone:

- Meditation helps quiet the mind, regardless of external circumstances
- Avoid unnecessary complexities and you'll be calmer
- A simple, purposeful life reduces anxiety and helps clear thinking

When the lecture concluded, Julia approached Alexandra, expressing gratitude spontaneously, sensing an inexplicable connection. Before she could explore this feeling further, a friendly staff member appeared, a woman dressed in soft, light-colored clothes, her smile gentle and genuine. She invited Julia on a quick tour of the Center.

The tour culminated on the mezzanine in the silence room. Stepping inside was like entering another world, an oasis of stillness amidst Manhattan's relentless chaos and noise.

Her bare feet sank slightly into the soft white carpet, inviting her to slow down and savor the moment. A sanctuary where time stood still, and the sense of self dissolved into pure light. The walls, a gentle creme-white, seemed to radiate serenity, as though they had absorbed the vibes of peace of meditating minds over many years. The silence felt almost sacred.

A few white chairs and a row of floor cushions, their presence inviting you into an unspoken reverence for the moments about to unfold.

Her eyes were drawn to the painting that adorned the focal wall. A large, diamond shaped square, with at its heart glowing a source of gentle white light, like a whisper from eternity. Delicate, almost imperceptible rays radiated out of this central point of light. There was something refined and special about this image of light, its silent energy reaching out touching something deep within her, cradling her in its embrace. The noise of Manhattan was absent, even the chatter of her mind grew still, hushed by the room's aura.

As Julia lowered herself onto a floor cushion, the silence wrapped around her like a comforting shawl. She closed her eyes, and the light from the painting lingered behind her lids. She felt herself starting to let go, of the city, of the world, of herself, until all that remained was light and quiet.

And in the silence, she felt a presence. Someone invisible and benevolent, so loving, peaceful, invisible yet undeniably real.

God?

Julia would describe herself as an atheist, but this was the only word that popped in her mind. Though she couldn't explain it, she surrendered to the warmth of this divine presence. As though she had finally found home.

Emerging from the silence room, she carried a new understanding: she was not merely a body, but a spiritual being of light connected to something greater. And in that realization, she felt free.

She walked out of the Meditation Center in a daze, somewhat shaken about but in a pleasant way. She made her way home feeling as if a more refined part of her woke up and was trying to find its way to the surface. "I was never superstitious or religious and now I feel as if touched by something transcendent," she thought. Everything appeared different, gross, and less important. Entering her apartment, the place felt so strange, like it was someone else's place. In an attempt to shake off these unfamiliar feelings, she switched on the television, however nothing was interesting enough to hold her attention.

It was only when she reached for her phone that she realized the extent of her absorption. The device, still set to silent mode, had several missed calls and messages from Nicolas. She quickly called him.

"Where are you? Are you okay? We are all here waiting for you and worried."

"I am home," she said. "I was at the place we were supposed to meet, the Meditation Center and that lecture on Happiness. It was an inexplicable and yet wonderful experience. But you never came. What happened?"

"Where were you?" Nicolas was surprised. "Meditation Center? Never heard of that place. I am waiting for you at this new Korean restaurant on Fifth Avenue. Can you still come, ... quickly? We are all here."

Julia looked surprised at her phone. Where had she been?

"Where are you?" she said to Nicolas. Can you send the address again? I must have gone to the wrong place."

In a daze she put on her shoes and coat again and took a taxi to the address that Nicolas texted her. "309 Fifth Ave," he had repeated it three times. But the previous address he had sent her was 306 Fifth Ave.

She stepped into the fancy surroundings of the restaurant and was greeted by a waiter who took her to a private room. Nicolas was extra sweet and loving and friends greeted her with warmth and joy. A big birthday cake came out and they sang and toasted and all shared nice things about her. Julia just let it all wash over her. These were her people, she loved them, they loved her. She found herself between the chatter and celebration, and the lingering echo of that light and stillness from earlier that night. Though surrounded by love and laughter, she could not help her thoughts being pulled back to that silence room, to a promise of something she could not grasp with her reason but could not resist either.

At midnight the party was over, and Nicolas brought her home. It was only after he bid her farewell, his duties at the hospital calling him away once more, that Julia found herself alone again with her thoughts. Collapsing onto her sofa, she was consumed by the memory of that light-filled space pulling her like a magnet. It was a wet, windy, and somehow cold New York September night, and she was shivering. She took a hot shower and lay down in her warm bed. Again, her thoughts were pulled back to that silence room, … and that invisible loving presence.

She opened the website of the Meditation Center on her phone, and the image of the same diamond shaped star-like light filled the screen with a red-orange golden-like glow. That same vibe from the silence room seemed to come through her phone and filled the atmosphere of her bedroom. She navigated to the guided meditations section, allowing the soothing voice to carry her away once more into the realm of stillness, timelessness, and light.

And as she lay there, bathing in the gentle light on her phone, Julia promised herself to learn about meditation. And she knew that this was only the beginning of something extraordinary.

That night, Julia dreamed.

She stood at a crossroads, darkness behind her, light ahead. Turning toward the shadows, familiar faces began to emerge, from past and present. Each figure drifted by like a soft echo from her life. Silently, warmly, they greeted her, offering smiles that held years of love, moments shared, memories treasured, some painful ones. Wordless greeting. Warmth and nostalgia filled her heart, mingling with a touch of longing.

Gradually, the faces faded, becoming transparent, until each one changed into a delicate, shimmering star. One by one, they took their place in a vast expanse, like fireflies in a golden-red sky, beyond the physical sky.

Julia, too, felt her body dissolving like the mist in the morning sun until she, too, was a star, a being of light, part of a family of living star-like beings. Immersed in an invisible dance of loving feelings.

When she awoke, her heart felt light, her mind clear. She rose from the bed and drew back the curtains, gazing out over Central Park from her 8th-floor window. Morning light spilled across the park below, illuminating people and cars moving along the avenue. Familiar scenes, dogs and their owners walking, others rushing with their bagpack and coffee in hand. It all looked so small down below and the height added to the feeling of emotional distance. All familiar, yet feeling different, like a scene in a theater, a stage with actors and props. The world seemed at once vibrant and strangely unreal. She stretched, trying to shake the feeling, but the sense of 'loving involvement but detached and free' lingered, leaving her strangely enough with a pleasant feeling of calm freedom.

Compelled, Julia reached into her bedside drawer, looking for a long-neglected diary. She hadn't written in ages, but today, words came freely, pouring from her mind to the page. In one seamless flow, she wrote:

Just When.
Looking at the many windings of fate across the horizon,
appearing incomprehensible and hazy.
The next plot,
Also seemed twisted and intricate.

And just when the winds were turning into a hurricane,
just when clouds seemed to be forever blocking the sun's light,
just when tangled thoughts started to become obsessive,
and a life of superficiality and commonness felt all-consuming...

Just then,
a soundless whisper touched my mind:

You are a guest in this world,
You are a guest in the body.
Remember...?

You are timeless...
You are invisible...
You are light!
Remember...! Remember....!

Julia looked at the paper. This was her? She felt content but also a bit unsure. While moving through her morning routine - coffee, shower, breakfast, news - a gentle pull remained, to the light-filled space she had glimpsed in her dream. Her heart held a new longing for that deeper peace.

CHAPTER 2

At Work

"Hey, what's going on in that dreamy head of yours?" Annie's voice sliced through the buzz of the office. Stylish and sharp in a red fitted skirt and matching blazer that mirrored her lively energy, her short black curls framed a confident face lit by a warm Latino glow. Julia snapped out of her reverie, the words from last night's meditation still lingering in her mind: *silence and light … timelessness … imperishable … soul … a traveler through time and space … a being of peace.*

Annie leaned closer, her curious eyes sparkling with mischief. "Are you in love or something? You've been sitting there all morning with that secretive smile. Spill it!"

Julia blinked and gave a soft laugh, but her focus remained elsewhere, without engaging in a conversation with Annie, who walked away to the coffee station.

The mundane rhythm of work, usually engaging, seemed faint and distant. She looked at the forms and spreadsheets on her computer, a retirement investment plan for Mary, a new client. Julia was usually meticulous, diving into her work with enthusiasm, but today her heart wasn't in it.

Mary, a 45-year-old professional, had come to the bank seeking clarity about her financial future. She was hoping to retire at 65 with $1.5 million in savings. Mary was willing to invest $50,000 of her savings and contribute $1,000 monthly toward retirement.

Julia mapped out a plan: recommendations for a balanced portfolio, an individual retirement account and keeping an emergency fund.

Normally, Julia would feel a sense of accomplishment, helping clients chart their financial paths was something she loved, but today, the task felt routine, almost mechanical.

"Julia? Earth to Julia?" Annie prodded again. Julia smiled at her friend/colleague, brushing away the haze of her thoughts. "I'm fine, Annie. I just had some intriguing experiences last night."

Annie rolled her eyes playfully. "Well, you'd better snap out of it before the boss catches you daydreaming!"

As Annie walked away, Julia's thoughts drifted back to last night's: *"We have 30,000 thoughts a day. How many of them enrich us or inspire us? Your thoughts shape your mood, your actions, and the energy you bring to your day."* The simplicity of it resonated with Julia, like a new lens through which to view her life.

Her gaze returned to the computer screen, but the words and numbers blurred. She took a deep breath and let a different thought settle: *"Viewing yourself as a guest in this world helps to remain free from unrealistic expectations and dependencies. Each moment, each interaction, is a gift. What would this workday look like if I saw it as a gift?"*

As often for lunch, Julia and Annie sat across from each other at their favorite lunchroom. They were colleagues, and had grown into friends. The energy felt light but curious. Annie leaned over, eyes sparkling with interest.

"Alright, Julia, spill it. What's this 'amazing experience' you mentioned earlier? Don't leave me hanging."

Julia smiled, folding the napkin in her lap. "Well, it's hard to put into words, but last night, I attended this lecture and meditation session. It was about exploring the habits of happiness and the idea that peace and happiness come from within, not from anything external."

Annie raised an eyebrow. "Sounds deep. What exactly did they say?"

Julia sipped her tea and continued, "One of the things that stuck with me was this idea that our thoughts are like seeds. If we plant thoughts that are benevolent and positive, they will positively influence our feelings, actions, and interactions." Julia paused, as if to let the meaning of this sink in. "I am realizing how much time I spend worrying and having thoughts that are useless."

Annie nodded slowly. "Okay, that's interesting. But isn't it hard to stay positive all the time?"

Julia laughed gently. "Oh, it did not feel like ignoring challenges. It's more like... having a trustee attitude. You appreciate everything, using it appropriately without clinging to it. I've been trying to keep that perspective this morning, and I feel a pleasant lightness."

Annie tilted her head, intrigued but skeptical. "So, do you really feel... different?"

"I do," Julia said honestly. "I'm noticing little things more, like how peaceful it feels just sitting here with you, talking."

Annie smiled. "Alright, Julia the philosopher. Maybe you can share some of these habits with me sometime."

The office chatter and the distant clacking of keyboards filled the air as Julia returned to her desk after lunch. Annie's curiosity was piqued but laced with skepticism, she couldn't quite reconcile the Julia she knew, practical, driven, and unrelentingly dependable, with this newfound dreamy demeanor.

The usual office work began to pick up again, phone calls, emails flooding in, and she had three meetings with clients. She consciously paused every so often to take a deep breath and center herself, recalling the words from last night: *"You are a being of peace."*

The afternoon stretched on, Julia glanced at her screen. The opened files blinked back at her, their columns of figures as precise and cold as ever. She had some more investment plans to draft, outlining options in greater detail for several clients. She performed each one with precision but without the usual fervor.

Every now and then, her thoughts drifted again to the silence room, the luminous painting, the peaceful vibe that left only the stillness in her head. She had sat there, feeling a profoundly comforting quietude. The world outside, with its relentless pace and clamor, had felt a universe away.

Even now, in the middle of Manhattan's bustling chaos, the memory of that stillness enveloped her like a protective cocoon.

And Alexandra's eyes, so clear, as if they knew the answers to life's riddles. There had also been a picture of a man who was the founder of the institution. His eyes seemed deep and non judgmental, as if he loved everyone in the whole world like his family. Those eyes had something non-human about them. Unearthly, divine. As if someone else was borrowing those eyes. Someone selfless and pure, someone supremely wise and peaceful. Someone who makes you feel silent and safe.

"Julia," came a sharp voice, snapping her back to the present. It was her manager, Mr. Benson, a tall African-American man with an impeccably pressed shirt, sleek tie, and the composed alertness of someone who noticed everything. His expression was cool, professional, yet edged with the sharp intelligence that kept the whole floor on its toes. "Did you finalize the projections for the Davis account?"

"Yes, it's in your inbox," Julia replied, her voice steady but softer than usual. She watched as he nodded and walked away, feeling no usual surge of relief nor accomplishment. Instead, she felt oddly detached, as though she was observing her own life from a distance.

When the clock struck 5 pm, Julia did something she hadn't done in a very long time: she shut down her computer on time. She closed her laptop and tidied her desk. No lingering over unfinished tasks, no staying late to perfect a client presentation. She gathered her things and stood up, her movements deliberate and unhurried.

Annie looked up from her cubicle, noticing this deviation from Julia's norm.

"Leaving on time? Is this the same Julia who practically lives here?" Annie teased.

Julia chuckled. "The emails will still be here tomorrow."

Annie smiled, shaking her head. "Whatever happened last night really got to you, huh?"

Julia paused, a contented expression on her face. "Maybe it did. See you tomorrow, Annie."

"Wait" Annie said "I'll walk out with you. I want to buy something to eat for later because I will be in for a while longer. I have to finish two more reports."

As they walked out, Annie started her interrogation. "So, what is this meditation thing really about? You're not... joining a cult, are you?"

Julia's eyes widened. "It's just... a space to breathe, to think about things differently. Last night, they talked about thoughts, how they shape everything. How our thoughts are our greatest treasure, our greatest assets. How much do we value this treasure? How careful are we with this wealth? It made me realize how much noise and junk we carry around in our heads."

Annie frowned. "Noise and junk?"

"Yes, like mental clutter," Julia said. "All the worries, judgments, and unnecessary chatter. What if we cleared some of that out? What if we focused on empowering and more beautiful thoughts?"

Annie seemed to mull this over as they descended the stairs. "I'll admit, you do seem… calmer. Less frazzled."

"I just went to one lecture," Julia said. "They have a meditation course for which I signed up. Do you want to come with me?"

Annie laughed. "Don't push it. Let me get used to this different you first."

They parted ways outside the building, and as Julia walked to the subway, she felt a quiet satisfaction. The day had been ordinary in its tasks but extraordinary in how light and calm she felt inside. She was not running on autopilot.

Nicolas had night and weekend shifts for the rest of the week. So they probably won't meet until Sunday evening. Julia noticed that she did not feel the usual disappointment and unease she would feel when Nic was so occupied with work. She loved being with him, but today she looked forward to being by herself. Enjoying the company of her own thoughts. Tonight, she would sit in her apartment, light a candle, and revisit the stillness. And perhaps, she would carry a little more of that peace into the days to come.

CHAPTER 3

Awakening to Light

Two weeks after her first accidental visit, Julia found herself once more crossing the threshold of the Meditation Center. The space welcomed her like an old friend, serene and quietly luminous. The air was laced with a delicate hint of eucalyptus and something floral, as if the atmosphere itself had been washed clean.

A few familiar faces nodded in greeting, their expressions warm but unobtrusive. Julia slipped into a seat near the back, her mind unusually still, as if some inner clock had slowed its ticking. Around her, about thirty others gathered, along with a few quiet faces on Zoom on a screen on the wall.

The course was about to begin, and though Julia had gone about her day as normal, a subtle anticipation had been growing inside her all morning. Not nervous but more like the flutter of a sail catching a soft new wind.

The facilitator, Claire, entered the room like a soft breeze. She was in her forties, though she carried herself with the lightness of someone younger, brown hair tied back, peaceful eyes, and a quiet elegance that seemed to move with her. Her presence, neither commanding nor dramatic, yet holding the space completely through her calm, her clarity, and a warmth that felt lived, not practiced.

"Let's begin," Claire said simply, her voice like a hand reaching out to gather them all into a circle of stillness.

She invited them into meditation with the gentle confidence of someone who knew the path herself.

"Withdraw your attention from the world outside," Claire's voice guided. "Gently allow the noise and the scenes of the day to fade from your mind."

Julia followed the suggestion, feeling the familiar busy-ness of her mind loosening its grip. She became aware of the weight of the body in the chair, the rhythm of her breath moving like a slow tide in and out.

"Now," Claire continued, "become aware of the one who experiences the body and the bodily sensations, the one behind the senses. The one listening through the ears, seeing through the eyes, thinking through the mind. The invisible experiencer, the being of consciousness."

A pause, and then, more softly: "Not the body... but the being using the body...

"In the mind, hold the image of light, like a star" Claire said, "a peaceful presence."

Envisioning a sparkling light shining at the center of her forehead, Julia drifted into a state of quiet where thought stilled and feelings were benevolent. No longer bound by the senses, she felt cocooned in silence and light. She just sat there in that awareness, a being made of light, still and timeless.

When Claire ended the meditation, the room seemed wrapped in a softer, finer atmosphere. She smiled warmly as she spoke again.

"Meditation," she said, "is about remembering the real self, the invisible being of consciousness, the soul."

Her words were simple, but they landed somewhere deep in Julia's mind.

"We go through life clinging to many labels, our name, gender, job, possessions, etc. We build castles on these 'limited' identities. Meditation reminds us: the real I is non-physical. We are spiritual beings, souls. Immortal, peaceful, and free. Everything else is temporary."

Not the body...
but the being using the body...

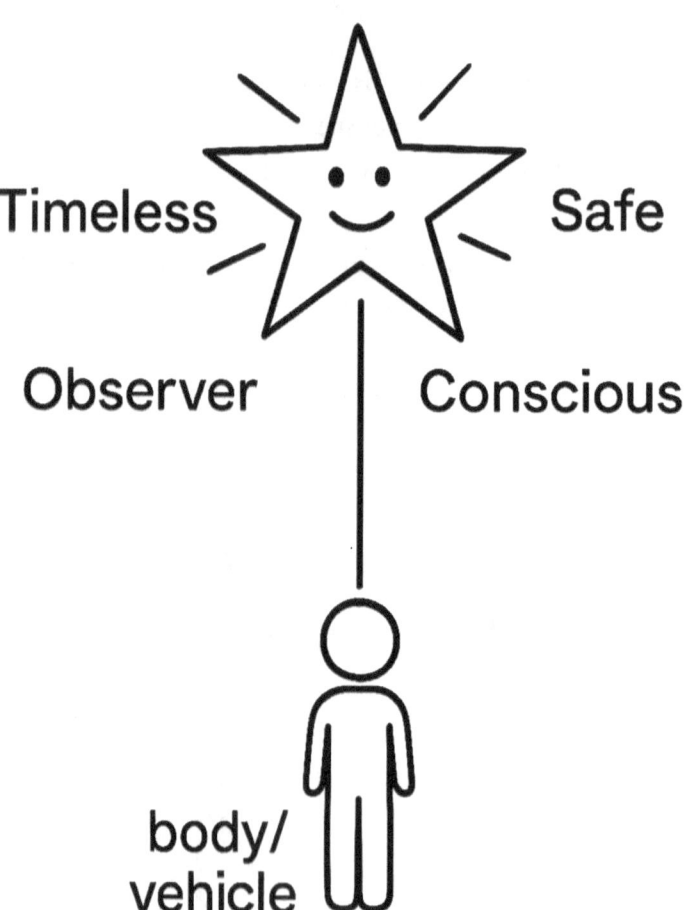

Imperishable being

Timeless

Safe

Observer

Conscious

body/
vehicle

Claire paused for a few seconds.

"We play many roles in this drama of human life. But when the body is laid down at the end of the play, the invisible actor, the soul, moves on."

The participants listened intently, each absorbing it in their own way. Some shifted in their chairs. Some leaned forward. Others closed their eyes again, as if trying to hold the feelings.

A man near the front raised his hand, his brow furrowed. "So... am I not my body, my job? How do I live practically if I'm not these things?"

Claire's smile deepened, touched with understanding.

"Of course, you honor your responsibilities," she said. "You care for your body, your loved ones, your work. But you do it with a deeper awareness that you are not defined by these things. You are the one using them, the one experiencing them. A soul playing out a role, but not limited by it."

She paused, as if inviting them to reflect on the sense and the freedom of that idea.

Then, with the same calmness, she led them into a second meditation.

"Aim to keep your eyes open and simply soften your gaze. Let the body relax. Let the mind quiet."

Her voice lowered to a near whisper.

"Feel yourself... the real you... as a sparkling living light. An eternal being of consciousness. The one who experiences life, is not the body, not the roles, not the possessions, but the invisible being of consciousness behind it all."

Julia closed her eyes because she felt it easier to concentrate, slipping easily into the invitation. Again, she pictured the self as a sparkling star behind her eyes. A peaceful observer, an invisible experiencer, untouched by the shifting drama of life.

"Timeless... gentle... free," Claire's voice echoed in the background.

The meditation unfolded like a soft tide over the room. It was not about erasing the world, Julia realized, it was about seeing it differently. About seeing herself differently. Not entangled. Not burdened. Simple and calm.

When the session ended, a few shared. Some spoke about restlessness, others about fleeting glimpses of stillness. One said that they could concentrate better with eyes closed. Claire listened to all of it with the same unwavering patience.

As Julia walked out into the cool Manhattan night, she carried a brightness inside her, a quiet memory stirring back to life.

Outside, the city lights blinked in soft patches across the darkening streets, but Julia hardly noticed them. She walked slowly, feeling the cool wind in her face, the lesson echoing in her mind.

People bustled past, taxis rumbled by, neon signs flickered against windows, and yet she moved through it all with a strange new detachment, like a traveler wandering through a colorful dream.

Not the roles... not the possessions... not even the body. The real 'I' is living light.

The words circled gently within her, making her feel such lightness, as if an old, heavy coat was dropped. At a quiet corner, Julia paused under a streetlamp, watching the shadow of the body on the pavement. She really liked this idea of being light.

QR Code
Guided meditation: The Real Self

CHAPTER 4

The Guest

Some participants did not return after the first session. Perhaps the quiet introspection had been too much, or perhaps it wasn't what they had expected.

Those who did return settled again into the light-filled room. The buzz of life outside filtered faintly through the high windows. Inside, the sanctuary of the room felt untouched, as though it had its own serene rhythm. The noise, the lights, the gleaming towers, the urgency of Midtown Manhattan, all of it seemed to fall away at the entrance.

Julia observed the tapestry of stories gathered around her. They came from every corner of life: different ages, different cultures, different dreams and heartbreaks. Some were between jobs. Some were between relationships. A few perhaps between moments of hope and despair. Yet here they all were, drawn by something unspoken. A yearning maybe, a pull toward something more, a curiosity about something higher.

Claire stood at the front, her serene presence setting the tone. Her smile was warm, her eyes peaceful.

"Before we begin today," she said, "I'd love to hear your experiences since our first session. Did anyone experiment with the ideas or try meditation at home?"

There was a moment of hesitation, a rustling of thoughts searching for words. A man in a crisp suit raised his hand.

"I tried to be more attentive to my mind," he said. "At first, it was chaos, thoughts about work, deadlines, bills, arguments I'd had. But then... there were these moments, brief, where it felt like everything paused. It is hard to describe, but it felt... still."

A woman with bright pink hair spoke up next. "For me it was frustrating," she admitted. "I kept getting distracted. My phone buzzed, or my mind wandered to my emails. How do you stop that?"

Claire nodded, her expression empathetic.

"Our mind has grown used to wandering. Meditation is not about fighting that but just shifting your thoughts. It's about guiding our thoughts, gently and with clarity. Like a parent guiding a curious child that gets distracted easily. Every time the mind wanders, you just bring it back to some constructive thoughts or to thoughts of meditation, lovingly but decisively. That itself is practice."

There were nods around the room.

Another woman, her face weary but soft, shared, "I've been feeling so disconnected lately. But when I tried the meditation, just remembering I'm a soul, a spiritual being, not a body... I felt so calm. Just to begin to think of myself as light. It was so sooth-ing. Like I wasn't carrying so many burdens."

Claire smiled, acknowledging the woman while appreciating and encouraging her sharing.

She then spoke of her own early journey, how she had stum-bled into meditation. "What drew me in," she said, "was the fo-cus on myself. The calming down of my thoughts and the clarity it gives in taking decisions about everyday situations. And how it brings perspective and peace in our interactions with others. I began to stop cursing for example when someone cut me off in traffic or behaved rudely in any way. It started to feel silly and only upsetting to myself."

Her story was met with nods and a few chuckles. She spoke of simple, tangible changes, her experiments with vegetarianism as her contribution to peace and non-violence, her practices of seeing all as part of one human family, appreciating the miracle of the body and nature at large.

Claire went on. "Let's take a moment to reflect on the essence of 'who we are.' To meditate is to recognize the difference bet-ween who we are and who we have come to believe we are." She paused briefly, then continued. "When we operate from what we call the 'false identity' or 'ego,' we identify with roles, possessions, appearance, etc. We believe, 'I am this body,' 'I am this job,' or 'I am this relationship.' This is called 'body-consciousness.' It starts with being impressed and attracted. Then we (unconsciously) feel we need and get dependent. And a false sense of ownership and/or neediness emerges. This gives rise to insecurities and fear,

fear of losing, of missing out, of losing our value and respect, of losing what we believe defines us."

Julia found herself leaning slightly forward, her pen poised but unmoving. She didn't want to miss a word.

"In contrast," she went on, "soul-consciousness is the awareness that I am a being of light. Eternal. Imperishable. A spiritual being. A guest in this body, a visitor in this physical world. Timeless. Safe. Immortal even though the body is not." She paused, letting the words settle like soft snow.

Claire drew a simple sketch on the board: a star above a stick figure.

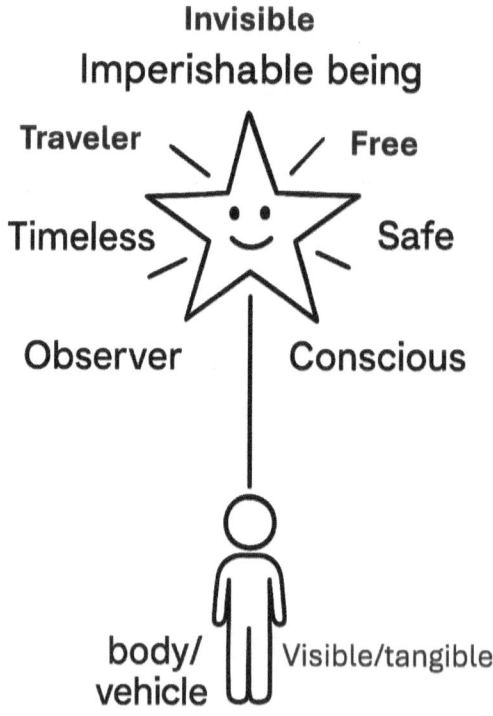

Invisible
Imperishable being

Traveler   **Free**

Timeless   **Safe**

Observer   **Conscious**

body/   Visible/tangible
vehicle

"You are a spiritual being, a being of consciousness. Symbolized by light. An invisible traveler, who uses the body as a temporary vehicle. Fully engaged, but free."

"As a guest," Claire's voice became softer, "as travelers we own nothing, and therefore we can't lose anything. Feel the freedom of this awareness. Every moment and every interaction become gifts."

Someone raised a hand. "But what about responsibilities? Jobs, family? How can we live like guests?"

Claire gently answered. "Being a guest doesn't mean ignoring or neglecting life. It means caring without clinging. Loving without fearing. Fulfilling your duties as a trustee with love and respect. Without needing to own. Contributing and cooperating without expectations or demands. And so, no burdens."

Julia felt touched. To love without clinging. To act without selfishness or neediness. It wasn't escape, but living while aware of a more subtle reality.

She felt a quiet inner joy rising. Her usual skepticism seemed to have melted away, replaced by a gentle delight she could not quite explain. It was as if, deep down, she had always known this, somehow.

As she reflected, Julia began to notice the countless images she held of herself. Little by little, she recognized the self-conceptions from which she operated. They were subtly shaping her thoughts, emotions, and attitudes. These roles and identities had been her constant companions.

She sat in silence, absorbed in these revelations, when a voice broke through her musing.

"So... am I not a man? Am I not an American? Am I not an engineer?" someone questioned, with a vibe of disbelief and cynicism.

Claire was not shaken, a gentle light in her eyes. "There was a time when you were not an engineer, but you were there! Everything physical is temporary, but the real 'I' is not. Even ideas, beliefs and tendencies change, end. But the being of consciousness, the soul, the real I, exists forever."

She went on, "when you say 'I', does it truly refer to the body or any of its parts? We never say, 'I am the ear' or 'I am the eye.' We don't say 'I am the skin,' so why should we define ourselves by the color of our skin, or the gender of the body, or the place of birth of the body?"

She paused. "The self may be aware of the body, aware of its form and its characteristics; we use the body to perform actions, to play different roles in this drama of human life, but does that mean that 'I' am the body? There will come a time when this body does not exist anymore. However, the real 'I', the being of consciousness, will continue to exist and continue on the journey."

Her voice softened, inviting them deeper. "We are bodiless, genderless beings of consciousness, using a body that carries its own gender, race, and unique characteristics."

"Let's have a meditation. I will speak some words as a suggested guidance for your thoughts. Just aim to hold those thoughts in your mind and surrender to the feelings they generate within you.

"Sit comfortably… and allow the body to relax. Try to keep the eyes open and just soften your gaze… Let go of any tension in the shoulders, the face, or the hands… Inhale slowly… and exhale… Become aware that the being is experiencing the body and the bodily sensations… Now, in the mind, hold the image of a tiny star, gentle light shining in the center of the forehead… This light is you… Not the roles, not the body, but the timeless being within… A spiritual being, free, pure, and innately divine… A sparkling living light… Feel the power of this thought.

"Now, think of the real self as a guest in this world, a guest in the body… temporarily visiting. Hold these thoughts in your mind.

"The soul, the invisible traveler, does not own the body nor anything else in this world. The awake soul experiences everything, appreciates without expectations, desires, or dependencies. With each breath, feel this lightness grow… One is free to simply be."

Julia let the words and feelings wash over her.

She pictured in her mind a tiny star, living light, safe, moving through the world without fear. A star, journeying through scenes, experiences, relationships, but never trapped by them. There was peace in this. A silent, profound freedom.

Claire continued, "Gently begin to see the truth of this. This body is not mine, it belongs to nature, to the elements of matter. It is a precious gift to use for a while. The soul passes through with elegance and gratitude. This thought creates space in the mind... free from stress, free from the burdens of ownership, free from fear of loss... The mind feels lighter... more peaceful... refined. Hold this... state of pure being. There is a subtle joy in knowing this. Let's use this awareness to guide us through the rest of the day."

Towards the end of the meditation, Julia had closed her eyes. She could focus better, she felt, feeling her way into the suggested thoughts. Claire invited everyone to slowly become aware again of their surroundings, aware of the bodily sensations. Julia felt as if everything had fallen away from her.

Around her, the participants were stirring, their faces calm, some even smiling softly. The classroom atmosphere felt so quiet and warm, as if time had stood still. Some opened their eyes reluctantly, others lingering a little longer in the quiet.

Claire concluded the session with a smile. "Meditation is not withdrawing from life. It's entering it wiser. It's playing the game of human life fully, having a broader perspective. Not an ego-based living with dependencies and anxieties."

They had all tasted this inner peace. But at times some had also felt a restlessness, a vague discomfort and distraction. One person's mind even wandered off completely, thinking of the pizza she would eat later. But the majority was able to surrender to the experience touching on a new sense of self... light, detached, an observer.

Julia felt like flying with her mind. She was quiet but had absorbed every word. She left in silence and walked home, getting the fresh cool air in her face. She tried to remember the meditations, the words spoken, and the feelings of lightness and serenity. She didn't yet know how much it would grow.

QR Code
Guided meditation: Guest Consciousness

CHAPTER 5

The Imperishable Soul

The city pulsed with life outside Julia's apartment, yet within its walls, there was a growing quietude. She had never imagined herself the type to sit still and to willingly reflect on the physical world, the non-physical, and invisible.

She was trying to meditate. *It wasn't about closing her eyes or forcing silence upon her mind,* Claire had explained. *Meditation is about holding spiritual thoughts in your mind, allowing the feelings connected with those thoughts to fill your mind. It wasn't about escaping reality, but broadening your understanding of self. Looking at self and life from a soul-based perspective instead of from an ego-based perspective. Instead of thinking of yourself as a mortal, human being, understanding and experiencing yourself to be an invisible and eternal being of consciousness, innately divine in nature. Using the image of light. Shifting from a body-conscious sense of self to a soul-conscious sense of self.*

Julia sat comfortably in her chair, her gaze resting on the city skyline. Meditation is a process of remembering, she mused. Remembering who you are, beyond the labels, beyond the roles. She rested her eyes on the horizon beyond Central Park and experimented with this thought.

I am not just Julia. Not a personal banker, not just a daughter, a friend, a girlfriend. I am something deeper, something constant, something untouched by time.

She recalled the steps to meditate.

Step One
Shift the attention from the body to the invisible being operating the body

Julia focused the attention on the self, the inner being, the living light behind the eyes… the one who sees through the eyes, who feels the bodily sensations, the one using the ears to hear. The invisible being of consciousness who observes and experiences.

She pictured it in her mind, a tiny, radiant star, operating from the forehead. A living light, steady, luminous, and eternal. Passing through this world, experiencing, playing the game of human life.

Step Two
Choose a specific theme

Julia had never considered the importance or even power of her thoughts. She had spent much of her working life thinking in numbers, equations, and outcomes. What if thoughts weren't just passing shadows, but tools to shape your feelings, mood, your actions and interactions? Deposits into my inner world, shaping how I feel?

She chose a theme for her thoughts: 'The Imperishable Soul.'

The real 'I' is eternal living light…

Bodies change, circumstances change, the world itself changes… but I remain.

The body is like a costume, which time will eventually wear away. Yet the soul, the actor, never dies. I enter the body, I play my part, and I leave. But my essence remains the same. Death belongs to the body, not to me. Just as you cannot burn light or break consciousness, so the soul cannot be destroyed. Imperishable, unborn, beyond decay.

This frees us from fear. Fear of loss, fear of endings, fear of the unknown. What can be lost if the essence of who I am remains? The story of life takes on a new shape. Relationships become meetings of eternal travelers. The past is a record of experience. And the future is simply another act in the play.

One starts to grasp eternity. I am not this fleeting moment; I am the one who witnesses moments. I am not the storm of emotions; I am the awareness that can watch them pass. The living light beyond the changes of time.

Step Three
Concentrate: hold only thoughts and images connected with the theme in your mind

Julia had always believed meditation was about emptying the mind, but she was discovering something new now. It wasn't about *trying to stop thoughts*, but about choosing which thoughts to hold in the mind.

She focused again.

The body changes... The seasons of life change... But the self... the soul... remains.

Imperishable... beyond birth... beyond death... An eternal traveler... taking costumes of matter... playing my part in the great drama of time... moving on after each scene.

The body belongs to the earth... but I belong to eternity.

No fire can burn... no storm can shake... no passage of time can erase me. I am an indestructible being of light.

The fears of endings dissolve... a living star, silent and constant... shining beyond the limits of time.

Step Four
Allow the feelings to fill your mind

She stayed in this experience for some time... in a state of deep peace and feelings of eternity and light.

The tension in her shoulders eased. The constant hum of urgency that followed her had quieted. A weightlessness settled over her.

She wasn't just thinking the thoughts anymore. She was *feeling* them.

Unburdened. Timeless. Living light.

QR Code
Guided meditation: The Traveler

STEPS TO MEDITATE

STEP ONE
Shift the attention
from the body to the
being operating the body

STEP TWO
Chose a specific
theme

STEP THREE
Concentrate: hold
only thoughts and
images connected with
the theme in your mind

STEP FOUR
Allow the feelings
to fill your mind

CHAPTER 6

Soul World and the Supreme Soul

The classroom glowed with a soft warmth that felt almost otherworldly. The walls, though modest, had a vibe of quiet energy. The late afternoon had folded into a calm evening.

Julia settled into her chair, both curious and expectant. The previous session had left her deeply moved, the thoughts and feelings around being a 'being of light.'

Tonight, the lesson promised to explore the broader dimension beyond the physical world. Claire started with a guided meditation.

Her voice filled the space and helped them all into a soothing calm. She revised the previous sessions and sketched the stick-figure again on the white board.

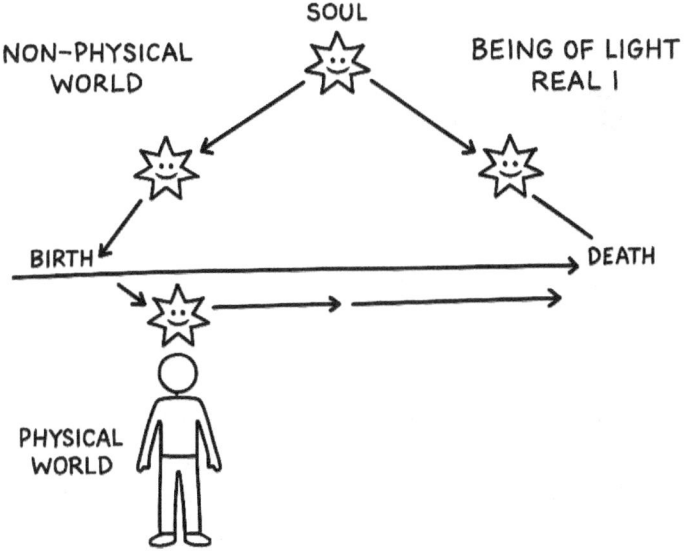

"The real 'I', the soul, is immortal, imperishable," Claire said gently. "A being who simply is, who needs nothing to exist, who does not age, does not perish. When in this awareness, and holding a traveler's perspective and attitude, our original nature of joy and love, of playful innocence, of purity and peace emerges."

THE ORIGINAL EXPERIENCE

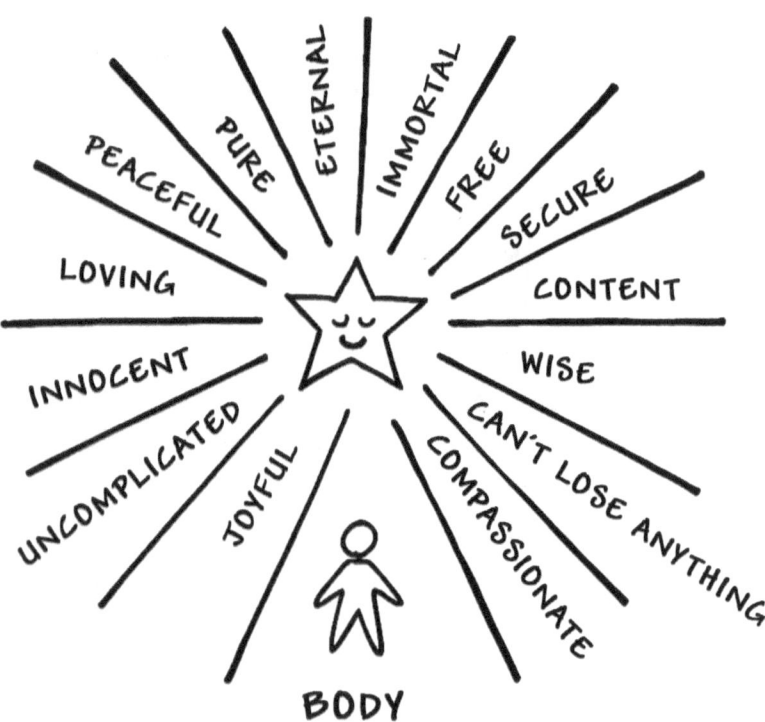

Claire explained that "Om Shanti," a phrase they seemed to use as a greeting, meant "I am a being of peace."

She paused, her eyes looking across the room. "The physical world is like a stage on which a play is acted out, the human world drama, with endless scenes and characters. But beyond this physical dimension there exists another dimension, the origin of the soul, the home of all the invisible travelers/players. A dimension untouched by time, sound, or change. This is the Home of souls."

Julia leaned forward, captivated. While she was talking, Claire enhanced the sketch on the white board with a line indicating the soul world beyond, above.

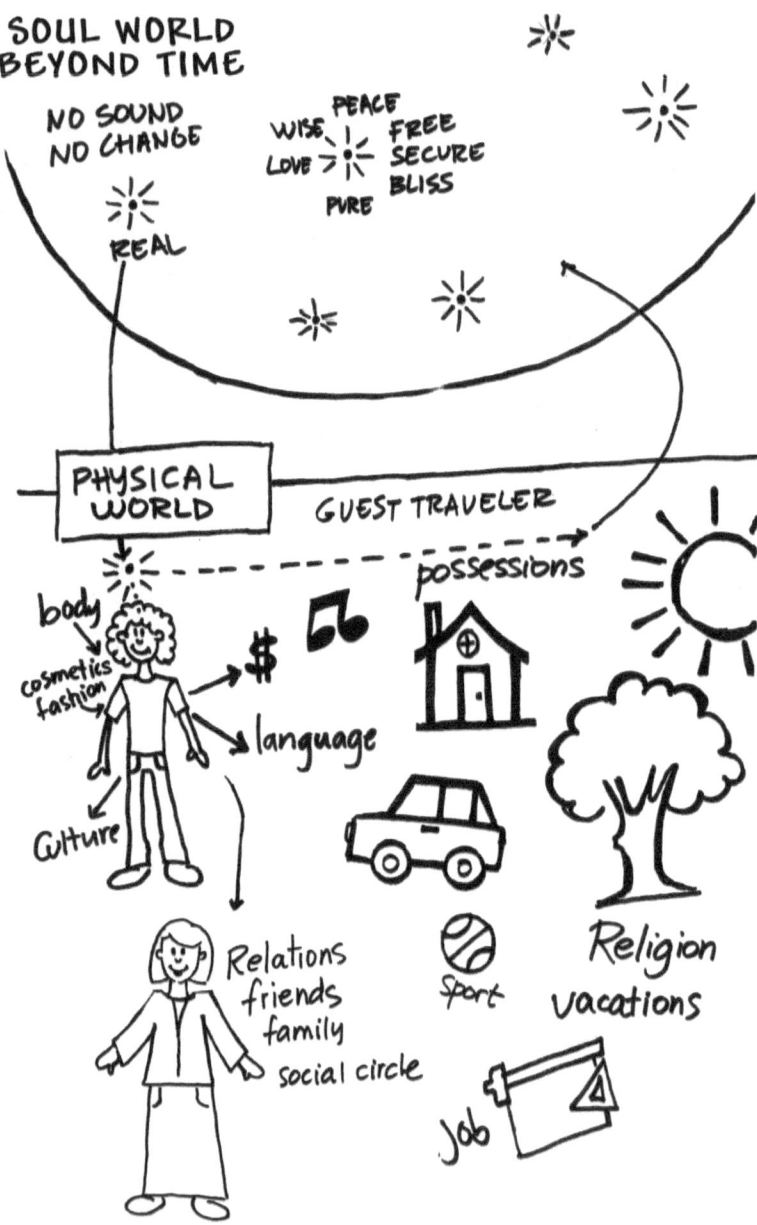

Julia closed her eyes. A Home beyond time? A dimension of silence and light? Was that what she had glimpsed in her dream the other night? That golden sky filled with living stars, and an overwhelming sense of belonging.

"In meditation," Claire continued with her gentle soothing voice, "we can shift our attention away from this physical world and turn our attention to the Home, a world of stillness. It can be experienced as a sky beyond the physical sky, a vast expanse of red-golden light. The residence of the family of souls, tiny conscious stars. This is the eternal world of our origin. It is here that we are truly ourselves, free of roles, free of masks, bodiless, egoless and viceless. It is here that we, souls, eternally belong."

Julia closed her eyes again, trying to perceive this dimension beyond, described as an expanse of endless light and silence. The very idea of an imperishable and pure 'world' that is Home was enough to lift the weight from her shoulders, as if her heart was sighing with relief.

"And in this Home," Claire said, her voice softening further, "resides the Supreme Soul, the eternal Parent of all souls. The Supreme does not have a physical form, but is also like a radiant star of light, pure, bodiless, and limitless in love and wisdom. The Supreme is like an Ocean of everything good: supreme wisdom, peace, and bliss. We can perceive the presence and mental company of the Supreme. Experience a relationship with God, soul to Supreme Soul."

Claire paused, allowing the words to settle. Julia's mind swirled with questions and wonder. As a little girl she used to believe and even talked to God privately. But she had thought of God as abstract and even unknowable. However, since college she had taken the position of atheism. And here this woman was talking about God in such a personal and intimate way, so close. And with such confidence. You could see that she was experiencing closeness with the Supreme. Her face sometimes glowed with a refined vibe that appeared almost otherworldly.

"The Supreme Soul," Claire continued, "is like the most perfect Parent, offering us every relationship we could ever need, a Teacher, a Friend, a Guide, a Companion, even a Beloved. In this bond, there are no conditions, no demands, only pure belonging, respect, recognition of the beauty and greatness of the soul, and trust."

Julia felt a quiet enthusiasm. The idea of such a bond with God awakened a sweet hope and relief, in the inner recesses of her mind she had quietly felt that such a relationship with the Divine must be possible although she had never quite been able to name. And over time she had just dismissed the whole 'idea' of God.

Claire's voice carried a steadiness and certainty as she continued, her gaze moving across the room. "From the eternal Home, the soul enters the dimension of matter, of sound, of action, of change. Arriving as a visitor, borrowing a body, stepping onto the vast stage of the physical world. But this journey is not meant to be a burden; it is more like an extra gift. The drama of life, with all its moments, its stories, its encounters, is a journey to be experienced, a game to be played, a treasure to be discovered."

She let the words settle.

"The invisible traveler is always safe, imperishable. Just like an actor playing out his part in a film" she continued, her tone warm. "No matter what happens here, no matter what scenes unfold, the spiritual truth about who we are remains unchanged. The Home is eternal. The connection with the Supreme is eternal. The soul belongs to a realm of stillness and pure light."

Julia, listening intently, felt as if she was being reminded of something she had known but somehow forgotten.

Claire smiled softly, as if sensing the unspoken thoughts moving through the room.

"The traveler, the soul, only needs to remember. To awaken from forgetfulness and return to that state of knowing. And this," she said, her voice lowering into something almost like a whisper, "is what meditation is about.

"Let us do a meditation using the four steps mentioned before. And in this meditation let's explore the home of souls."

Claire closed her eyes for a moment as if to withdraw her attention even more from the physical and tune into the invisible and timeless, … and then she began.

"Step 1: Remind yourself of the beautiful spiritual truth about yourself. Shift your attention from the physical to the invisible.

The soul is the invisible traveler, an invisible experiencer. Using the image of a tiny star to symbolize the soul."

Julia followed the guidance, and began to feel her thoughts grow quiet. Even though it was encouraged to keep the eyes open, she felt more easily concentrated with her eyes closed.

"Step 2: The Home of the soul is that dimension of silence and light, beyond the world of matter. Aim for 100% concentration."

Julia tried to concentrate. Seeing in her mind a light-filled expanse, like a sky beyond the sky of clouds. And the expanse was so vast that in comparison the physical world including her body appeared small and gradually started fading the distance. She felt as an observer of it all, floating, weightless, free from distraction. And the physical world disappeared completely from her mind. She was light... just light, immersed in silence and light.

She heard Claire say: "If other thoughts intrude, just gently come back to that golden sky. A vast expanse of light, limitless, still, timeless, and welcoming. A space filled with vibes of supreme love. Vibes of benevolence, of family, of being loved, and feeling safe."

Julia just let her mind be carried by the meaning of guiding words.

"Step 3: Concentrate. Engage your mind in that home of souls. See and experience the details.

"In our natural state in the Home there is selflessness. Being carefree, innocent, child-like and God-like. Free from needs and no-one ever can be lost. All are dearly loved brothers, family. Immortal beings. All are loved by God, and free to be in God's company. This is the Home of peace, the Home of eternity.

"Let any stray thoughts pass gently," Claire added, "and return your mind to this realm beyond. Immerse the mind in this stillness, ... in this silence, ... in this light, ... in this feeling of being safe forever.

"Step 4: Allow the feelings to fill your mind. Experience the truth of this. Feel it as natural. Allow those soul-conscious feelings to fully emerge and familiarize your mind with feelings like these.

"Now," Claire said after a moment, "notice the calm it brings, the stillness. Feel the warmth of that golden light, the peace of being in your true Home.

"Can you sense the silence? The welcoming vibrations? There's a freedom, a subtlety and a sense of being at home."

Julia exhaled deeply. She felt so peaceful.

As the silence stretched, Julia finally opened her eyes and met Claire's gaze. "That was... powerful," she murmured. Her palms were warm, slightly damp, but she hadn't moved. Her jaw, always clenched by habit, had softened without her noticing. She became aware of the others around. She just assumed, by their silence, that they had all also been immersed in this sweet peace.

Claire smiled. "Did you get a taste of the higher self and what lies beyond the world of the senses." Julia nodded. She had definitely glimpsed something she had not experienced before.

When she stepped out into the Manhattan night, the lights of the city seemed softer, the sounds less intrusive. She felt as though she carried her home with her, a sanctuary that no outside chaos could touch. And with that, she felt an enduring, unshakable peace.

QR Code
Guided meditation: The Soul World

QR Code
Guided meditation: The Supreme Soul

QR Code
Guided meditation: Beings of Light

CHAPTER 7

On the Train

The rhythmic noise of the train filled the air, punctuated by the occasional clatter of wheels on the tracks. Julia and Nicolas sat side by side, their weekend bags tucked neatly above them. He was tall, dark-haired, with the kind of quiet masculinity that needed no attention, his features held a trace of his native American heritage. The afternoon light streamed through the windows, painting warm patterns on their faces.

Nicolas leaned back in his seat, loosening the tension that had built up from the past week. He looked over at Julia, who sat quietly, gazing out of the window. Something about her felt different, as though a veil of calm had settled over her, a softness that both intrigued and comforted him.

"You've been very quiet," Nicolas said, breaking the silence. "Not that I'm complaining, but it's unlike you. What's on your mind?"

Julia turned her head toward him, her eyes thoughtful. "Oh, just thinking," she said, her tone distant yet warm. "You've had a tough week, haven't you?"

He exhaled deeply, running a hand through his dark hair. "Yes, I lost two patients. Young ones, too. Every time it happens, it still hits hard." He paused, his eyes wandering to the view outside. "I'm looking forward to this weekend. Maybe we can go hiking, get some fresh air and clear my mind. Nature always has a way of resetting things for me."

Julia nodded. "It's good to have that. A way to find balance."

They fell into a comfortable silence, the train rocking gently as it sped along. Nicolas studied her, sensing there was more she wasn't saying. "You seem... different," he said after a moment. "Peaceful, almost. Did something happen?"

Julia smiled softly. "I've been doing this meditation course. Remember that place I accidentally went to on my birthday, the Meditation Center? I decided to give it a try. I did three lessons this week while you were on night shifts this week."

Nicolas raised an eyebrow. "Really? I mean, you had mentioned it and I'm glad you like it, but I didn't see that coming. You've always been pretty skeptical about anything spiritual."

"I know," she admitted, laughing lightly. "I didn't expect it either. But it's not what I thought it would be. It's... different. Not about rituals and more about understanding myself, my thoughts. They talked about the Soul World, this place beyond the physical, and about God in a way I've never heard before. It's got me thinking."

Nicolas leaned forward, intrigued. "What'd you mean? What'd they say about God?"

Julia hesitated, searching for the right words. "They described God as a being of light, completely beyond the physical world. Not a figure in the sky or some abstract idea, but someone real, not a human being but more like an invisible benevolent presence, and personal. It's hard to explain, but it made sense in a way I didn't expect. Julia paused for a minute and then said, "Do you think about God?"

Nicolas blinked, caught off guard.

He leaned back, folding his arms as he considered. "Honestly? I don't know. Part of me wants to believe in something greater, something beyond what we see and touch. But the rational part of me doesn't accept it. I've spent so much time studying the human heart and body, understanding its anatomy and physiology. It's hard to reconcile that with the stories I heard growing up."

Julia tilted her head. "What stories?"

A small smile touched his lips as memories surfaced. "My grandmother used to tell me about the Great Spirit when I was a young boy. She said he wasn't someone you could see but someone you could feel. She'd take me hiking in the Hudson Valley and tell me to listen to the silence, to meet the Great Spirit in solitude. She said you had to be... naked to meet God."

"Naked?" Julia repeated, her brow furrowing in curiosity.

"I think it was not literally meant, ... maybe," Nicolas said with a chuckle. He fell silent, trying to recall those memories.

"Maybe she meant without distractions," Julia suggested remembering the things she'd heard at the Center. "Without the noise of the world, the ego, the need to be someone, do something, or have something."

Nicolas nodded. "She'd described it as a 'solitary communion with the Unseen.'

I used to love those hikes, the way they'd made me feel connected to something bigger, … but, … after I went to High School and College I never knew how to make sense of it all. The education and career shaped me into someone so different from her world."

Julia nodded slowly. "Maybe that's what it means to be naked, to let go of all the identities we cling to. The titles, the acquired ideas and theories, the possessions, etc.. To just be... a soul. Pure and simple."

Her words hung in the air, resonating with Nicolas in a way he hadn't anticipated. He thought of his grandmother's quiet strength, her unwavering faith in something intangible yet profoundly real. "She always told me that strength comes from silence and solitude. That in silence and solitude you find inner power, that you can be self-composed, balanced, and unshaken by the world. She called it meeting God in your own way, without anyone in between."

Julia's gaze softened. "That sounds … beautiful. And true. I wonder if that's what the meditation is trying to teach me, how to connect with that silence, that strength."

Nicolas looked at her, touched by the softness and sincerity in her voice. "Maybe it is. Maybe it's worth exploring, even if it doesn't fit into the science-based model of the world that I'm used to."

The train slowed as it approached their station. Nicolas stared out the window, lost in thought. His grandmother's wisdom, so deeply rooted in her heritage, suddenly felt closer, more relevant. Julia's words had stirred something in him. A desire to bridge the gap between his rational mind and the quiet truths he had once felt in the mountains and in his grandmother's company. Nicolas glanced at Julia, her face glowing with quiet determination. He smiled, suspecting that this weekend would be more than just a visit home.

CHAPTER 8

Julia Callaghan and Nicolas Van Wyck

The train had pulled into Poughkeepsie, the nearest station to Hyde Park, just as the sun began to dip toward the horizon. Julia and Nicolas stepped on the platform, the crisp air nipping at their faces. The familiar hum of small-town life enveloped them, a far cry from the cacophony of Manhattan. Every two months, they'd make this trip, carving out a weekend to visit their families in Hyde Park. It had become a tradition, a shared rhythm amidst their bustling city lives. While Julia stayed at her parents' home and Nicolas at his, they always found time to connect during these weekends, whether it was over a hike on a beloved trail or meals with the family. As they walked toward the parking lot where Julia's father was waiting to pick her up, she glanced at Nicolas with a soft smile.

"I'll see you tomorrow morning for coffee?"

"Bright and early," he replied, giving her hand a quick squeeze before heading toward his mother's car.

They had grown up just a few streets apart in Hyde Park. Their connection had begun in their teens at Haviland Middle School, part of a close-knit circle of friends who spent long afternoons together. Despite the two-year age difference, Julia's quick wit and Nicolas' steady, kind demeanor drew them together. By the time she was a sophomore at FDR High School, they were inseparable, their young love blossoming through late-night calls, movies and shared milkshakes. Over time, the bond deepened, weathering college, careers, and the pull of adult responsibilities.

Their families, once connected only through their relationship, had grown genuinely close. Festive days were often shared, and milestones marked together in warm gatherings. Still, when they returned to Hyde Park, they slipped back into the rhythm of their separate family homes, a small way of honoring where they had come from.

Julia had always been an observer, curious, thoughtful, and attuned to others. Her life was shaped by two distinct cultures. Her mother, Elena, originally from Peru, had built a life in the U.S. from the ground up. After her father's passing, Elena had come to America, working first as a cleaner before building her own successful real estate business, a testament to her determination and hard work. A devoted Catholic, she sometimes worried about Julia's spiritual path, especially since Julia, when asked, often referred to herself as an atheist. Julia's father, Dan Callaghan, was a retired firefighter from the Bronx who had worked in Manhattan and served during 9/11.

He brought humor, warmth, and a love of hiking and storytelling to the family. Though once a practicing Catholic, he had long since drifted away from religion, instead embracing a quiet wisdom shaped by experience. Growing up between her mother's fierce determination and her father's gentle presence, Julia had developed a blend of ambition and sensitivity. Together, her parents raised three children in a loving, if occasionally chaotic, household.

After graduating from FDR High School, Julia went on to NYU to study economics and business accounting. Her talent and diligence carried her through various certifications in financial planning, and she built a career as a personal banker in Manhattan.

Though accomplished, she often felt unsure whether she truly belonged in the glamorous world of high finance. Her life in the city was secure. Her mother's smart investments had left her with a spacious apartment overlooking Central Park, a rare comfort in New York City. Though naturally shy, Julia drew people in with her warmth and sincerity. She kept a small circle of close friends, most of them more extroverted than she was. They'd often joke she was the quiet glue that kept everyone together.

Her relationship with Nicolas remained her sanctuary. He understood her in ways others didn't, their shared history creating a friendship that grounded them both. Still, Julia sometimes questioned whether she leaned on him too much. She wondered if she relied too heavily on his steadiness, allowing it to buffer her from the sharper edges of life.

As her father's car pulled into the driveway, Julia was greeted by a rush of familiarity. Her mother stood waiting at the door, arms crossed and eyes glowing as she called out, "Welcome home, mija!" (Spanish for 'my daughter'). Julia stepped into her mother's embrace, soft-voiced but full of feeling. Her father followed with her bags. Home, as ever, was a mix of love, warmth, and occasional frictions, familiar and grounding.

Meanwhile, Nicolas had walked over to his mother's car after saying goodbye to Julia. The chilled wind whispered through the trees as he slid into the passenger seat. His mother welcomed him with her characteristic warmth, and for a moment, he felt like a boy again, returning to something essential. Coming home to Hyde Park always brought a quiet kind of peace.

It wasn't just the slower pace or fresh air, it was the sense of belonging. The land held memories of childhood hikes, long conversations with his grandmother, and a closeness to the natural world that his life in Manhattan did not offer.

Nicolas had grown up surrounded by the natural beauty of the Hudson Valley. His father, James Van Wyck, a pilot for American Airlines, was a tall, composed man with roots in Dutch and Scottish heritage. Though often away on international routes, he had always been steady and dependable. Nicolas' mother, Caroline, had grown up on a Native American reservation and went on to become a history teacher. Her life was devoted to preserving and teaching Native American history through her work with local schools and museums.

The stories passed down from her and Nicolas' grandmother shaped his early worldview, tales of the Great Spirit, the sacredness of all life, and the dignity of silence and self-mastery.

His grandmother, a woman of quiet but formidable strength, had lived with them until he was 14. She had been a major influence on him. Born and raised on a Native American reservation, she'd carried the weight of her heritage with dignity and pride. Even in her eighties, she would take Nicolas hiking through the woods, pointing out herbs, birds, and streams, telling him stories of nature's spirit and the meaning of strength. Her teachings about emotional discipline and honoring all life lingered in his memory. "A man who cannot master his emotions or his desires, she once said, is like a tree without roots, easily swayed by the wind." Her words stayed with him, though for many years now, they felt more poetic ideals than practical truths.

When his grandmother passed away at 83, Nicolas felt a deep sorrow. Yet her voice, her stories, and her dignity had become part of the framework through which he understood life, something he was only now beginning to fully recognize.

Nicolas' life path had been one of discipline and pursuit. After high school, he studied economics at Columbia while completing his pre-med requirements. He went on to medical school at Stony Brook and then a cardiology fellowship at Harvard. Now, as a practicing cardiologist at NYU, he was seen as a success by all accounts. His apartment in Hoboken placed him within easy reach of the hospital and of Julia's apartment. Life was full, rewarding, but not without weight.

The COVID pandemic had left many invisible scars. As a young physician only months into his career, he had been thrust into a whirlwind of fear, loss, and exhaustion. The memories were etched into his mind, the weight of decisions, the helplessness in front of a new virus, the eyes of patients who had no one else but the doctors and nurses next to them. The camaraderie of his colleagues had helped, but the nightlife, the drinks, the fleeting release others found in distraction never brought him solace. What stayed with him were his grandmother's words, echoing through the exhaustion: dignity, respect for life, walk lightly. He had tried to keep going, tried to find balance. But sometimes, even now, he wasn't sure how to fully come home to himself.

Through all of it, Julia had been there. Her presence was steady, her love quiet and genuine. Though they didn't live together, their lives were deeply woven. Nicolas admired her intelligence, her discipline, and her honesty. He loved that she questioned things, that she never pretended to have it all figured out. In her presence, he felt like he didn't have to either.

This weekend, like so many before, had begun with a train ride and familiar greetings. But something felt different this time. Something new was quietly stirring.

CHAPTER 9

A Quiet Evening at Home

The kitchen smelled of roasted corn and sage as Nicolas leaned casually against the counter, watching his mother chop vegetables with the ease of someone who had done it a thousand times before. Outside, the evening light filtered through the window, painting the scene in warm yellows and orange. The house was quiet, except for the soft muffled sound of the stove vent and the occasional clink of a knife against the cutting board. His father was in the UK, flying one of his final transatlantic routes before retirement later this year, leaving the house to just the two of them.

Nicolas had always loved this kitchen. It was the heart of his childhood home, with its well-worn wooden table and mismatched chairs. The shelves were lined with jars of herbs, some gathered from the garden out back, others gifted by his grandmother long ago. He picked up a small jar labeled Sweetgrass. He rolled the sweetgrass jar between his hands slowly, like a memory he wasn't ready to let go of. He opened it, inhaling the faint, earthy scent that instantly brought him back to childhood. The scent clung to his skin, to something deeper than memory, something more like longing.

"Mom," he said suddenly, breaking the silence.

His mother turned, her gentle face framed by loose strands of hair. "Yes, sweetheart?"

He hesitated, holding the jar up. "Can we talk about Grandma? I've been thinking about her a lot lately."

His mother raised her eyebrows slightly, a smile tugging at her lips. "That's not something you bring up often lately," she said, her tone light but curious. "What's on your mind?"

He shrugged, trying to find the words. "I guess I've just been... remembering her. The stories she used to tell, the hikes we went on. How strong she was, even in her eighties. I mean, she could still out-hike me back then."

His mother chuckled softly as she wiped her hands on a towel. "Oh, she had the spirit of a warrior, that's for sure. Born in 1920, on the reservation. She grew up with so little, but she always said she was richer than anyone because she had the land, the essence of morality, and the stories of her people."

Nicolas pulled out a chair at the table, motioning for his mother to join him. She carried a bowl of squash to cut into smaller pieces and sat down, looking at him with a warmth that made him feel like a child again.

"Did she ever talk about what it was like growing up there?" he asked.

His mother nodded. "Oh, plenty. She used to say that the land taught her everything, patience, resilience, respect. She believed that every tree, every rock, every stream was alive and to be revered and respected. To her, the Great Spirit wasn't just someone you prayed to; you lived His laws and you saw His divinity in everything. She believed that nature reminded us of His beauty and magnificence. That present-day humans have lost their relationship with God because they have separated themselves from nature and even abused and destroyed nature. This of course includes our own body."

"That explains why she loved taking me hiking so much," Nicolas said, smiling faintly. "Do you remember how she'd pack those tiny sandwiches and a thermos of tea? She'd tell me about the Great Spirit, about how we're all connected."

His mother's eyes glistened as she laughed. "She was always teaching, even when you didn't realize it. She believed that nature could heal what people couldn't."

Nicolas hesitated before asking, "What about... the day she died? What was it like?"

His mother's smile softened into something more introspective. "She passed so peacefully, Nic. She was sitting in her favorite chair by the window, looking out at the garden. I went to bring her tea, and... she was just gone. No pain, no fear. She was ready. She always said she wanted to go like the setting sun, quietly, gracefully."

He nodded, absorbing the image. "She really lived by what she believed, didn't she? All the way to the end."

"She did," his mother said quietly. "And she left a piece of that wisdom with all of us. Especially you. She adored you, Nic."

They sat in silence for a moment, the weight of memory filling the space.

Finally, his mother stood up, finished the cooking, and began setting the table. The food was ready and with a hand gesture she invited Nicolas to serve himself. They both sat at the table and started eating.

"What's brought all this up now? Is everything okay?"

Nicolas leaned back in his chair, running a hand through his hair. "I am not really sure. Work's been... heavy. I lost two patients this week. I keep thinking about their families, about what they must be feeling. Then I remember Grandma, how she seemed to know something about life and death that I'm still trying to figure out."

His mother paused, she put down her fork, her face soft with understanding. "Tell me more," she said simply.

Nicolas pushed his plate a bit forward and rested his elbows on the table. His mother looked up at him, her brow furrowing slightly. "Yes?"

He hesitated, rubbing the back of his neck. "It's work... and everything that comes with it. After a tough week, sometimes the guys from the hospital, other doctors, nurses, others, they'll go out to blow off steam. Bars, clubs, whatever. I go with them sometimes. I try to fit in, let loose." His mother didn't interrupt, letting him find his words. "But it doesn't really help," he said. "It's just a distraction. Sure, in the moment, it feels like we're letting go of all the stress, having a good time. But afterward... I just feel worse. Empty. Like I've lost something, even though I was trying to feel better. Julia often comes with us, but it doesn't feel like she enjoys it, either."

She set down her spoon, turning to face him fully. Her expression was calm, thoughtful. "What do you think you've lost?"

He sighed. "I don't know... dignity, maybe? There's no self-control in those moments. Everyone's drinking too much, saying things they wouldn't normally say, acting like someone else. I sometimes even end up throwing up in a cab or waking up with a pounding headache, and I just think... what's the point?"

His mother nodded slowly. "You're not alone in feeling that way, Nic. A lot of people turn to things like that to cope with stress and even pain. But it sounds like it's not the kind of relief your heart is really looking for."

He looked at her, his shoulders tense. "So what am I supposed to do? Just keep carrying it all with no outlet?"

She smiled gently, her voice calm and steady. "Grandma used to say that real strength isn't about suppressing pain or trying to distract yourself. It's about holding it with grace, about honoring it as part of life's journey, and about learning the lesson that life is trying to teach you. She believed that self-control wasn't really about discipline, it was about dignity. About staying true to who you are, even when the world feels overwhelming."

He frowned, absorbing her words. "That's easier said than done."

"It is," she agreed. "But it's also freeing. She used to tell me that self-control is like a riverbank. Without it, the river, our emotions, our struggles, can flood and destroy everything in its path. But with it, the river can flow with purpose, with strength. It can nourish the land instead of tearing it apart."

Nicolas stared at the table, tracing the wood grain with his finger. "So what, I'm just supposed to stay home and meditate instead of going out with my friends?"

His mother chuckled softly, shaking her head. "Not necessarily, sweetheart. It's not about avoiding life. It's about being aware of what truly brings you peace and fulfillment. Maybe it's not the drinking or the partying, but something else or simpler. A walk in the park. Sport or hiking. Sitting with your thoughts. A good book. Having a good conversation. Sharing quiet time with someone you love."

"But it seems to work for others. Am I just... different?"

Her smile deepened, a hint of her mother's wisdom shining through. "You're not different, Nic. You're just listening to something deeper in yourself. Something your grandmother always knew was there. She believed that when we're true to our own spirit, we find a kind of peace that no drink or party could ever give us."

He glanced up at her, his expression uncertain. "Today, on the train Julia and I had a nice time. Initially we sat in silence, but then she said some interesting things. She has started with a meditation course. That's so unlike her. And she seemed more quiet than usual, but she had a certain calm contentment about her that almost made me jealous. I will ask her to go hiking tomorrow." He took out his phone and texted Julia.

They had finished dinner. Nicolas didn't have much appetite. They cleaned the table and washed the dishes together while continuing the conversation.

Nicolas really was in a talkative and sharing mood. He told her more stories from the hospital, and she shared more about his grandmother, her laughter, her stubbornness, her unwavering faith in the interconnectedness of life.

They moved to the living room and his mother sat down in her favorite chair and Nicolas made himself comfortable on the couch.

Then even his thoughts and the feelings from the Covid-pandemic time surged. He had not realized how much that still lived in him. The endless shifts during that time, the chaos of those early months, and the weight of decisions that felt impossible. He spoke of colleagues he'd lost, of the times he felt he'd failed, and of the quiet, unspoken strength he'd found in caring for patients when no one else could be with them.

"During that time," he said, his voice low, "I started seeing patients differently. Not just as bodies to heal, but as souls. It's hard to explain, but... it was like their spirit was the most real thing about them. And when I couldn't do anything else, I just tried to be there with them in those last moments, to honor their spirit."

His mother reached across from her chair, resting her hand on his. "That's beautiful, Nicolas. It sounds like you were exactly what they needed, even if it felt helpless." He nodded, his throat tightening. "But it doesn't make it easier, Mom. Sometimes it feels like such a heavy load to carry."

She squeezed his hand gently. Her voice soft, "You've done more good than you know. Try not to carry it as a burden. The blessings from all those you've helped are with you. Share it with God.

"You know," his mother said, settling back into her chair, "your grandmother never condemned or criticized people for their choices or weaknesses. She knew everyone has their own path. But she always said that the most rewarding path was the one where you could look back and feel proud of the way you walked it."

Nicolas leaned back on the couch, his eyes fixed on the ceiling. "I would like that," he admitted. "I would like to feel proud of how I'm living. I just feel puzzled sometimes and life can feel so superficial."

His mother reached for his hand, her grip warm and steady. "You're asking these questions, you're reflecting on what feels right and wrong for you... that's in the right direction. You don't have to have all the answers now. Keep listening to that part of you that longs for something deeper."

As they sat together in the quiet of the living room, Nicolas felt a flicker of hope and a renewed enthusiasm. He felt grateful, realizing his privileges, appreciating and respecting his mother's words, his grandmother, and the way she was and used to make him feel in her presence, the memories they shared. It didn't erase the weight he carried, but it somehow felt lighter, made it feel more like lessons then burdens.

The conversation continued late into the night. By the time Nicolas went to bed, he felt a warmth around his heart, a satisfaction that he had not felt in a long time. The heaviness had shifted. He fell asleep feeling at peace.

CHAPTER 10

Going Hiking

It had been an almost three hour drive to the Hudson Gorge Wilderness but Nicolas wanted to go to a special spot he had been with his grandmother several times, long ago. It was called 'Angel's Rest.'

The trail wound like a living thread through the heart of the Hudson Gorge Wilderness, weaving past towering pines and clusters of birch trees. The morning sunlight streamed through the canopy, painting the forest floor with shifting patterns of gold and shadows. The air was crisp, and each step seemed to sink them deeper into the silence of nature. The earth beneath their boots, the distant calls of birds, the gentle rustling of leaves, these sounds were a language of their own, inviting them to listen, to pause, to breathe. Nicolas led the way, his strides steady, yet unhurried, as though he knew this land intimately. Julia followed close behind, her breaths mingling with the soft rustle of leaves and the distant murmur of the river.

They had been here before, once or twice, but today felt different, charged with a quiet reverence. Nicolas had spoken earlier of a special place, a sanctuary his grandmother had cherished and used to take him to. "It was a spot tucked away from the world," he had said, "where the trees opened to reveal a breathtaking view of the Hudson River Gorge."

The trail twisted and turned with ease at first, leading them through dense thickets of pines, their dark green needles glistening like gems under the sun's embrace. Julia, breathing in the earthy scent, felt her body loosen with each step, her usual thoughts quieting as she focused solely on the path ahead. There was something sacred about these woods, something ancient in the way the trees arched overhead, their branches like outstretched arms offering a canopy of protection.

After some time, Nicolas led Julia off the main trail, turning onto a narrower path that wound its way upward. The incline was steeper here, the terrain more challenging, but there was a look of determination in his eyes, a quiet excitement that she could not help but feel too.

As the narrow path grew steeper, the forest grew quieter. Even the birds seemed to get enveloped by the silence, their songs fading into the stillness. Nicolas moved with the ease of someone who had walked it many times before. Julia paused to catch her breath, looking up at the rugged peaks that framed the sky. Nicolas turned, his dark eyes filled with encouragement.

"Not much farther," he said, offering his hand. His touch was firm but gentle, and Julia felt a flicker of gratitude for the way he always seemed to know when she needed support. They climbed, their breaths steady, the trail narrowing further until it opened onto a view that stole the breath from Julia's lungs.

The Hudson Gorge stretched out before them, vast and untamed, the river carving a silver ribbon through the expanse of emerald and russet trees. The cliffs rose sharply on either side, their faces etched with the marks of time, while the valley below seemed to hold the secrets of the earth. The sky, vast and cloudless, arched above them, holding everything in its quiet embrace. The silence here was profound, sacred. It felt as if the land itself was holding its breath, waiting for them to witness its beauty without interference.

The morning had slipped into a soft, golden afternoon as Nicolas gestured to a large, flat rock near the edge, offering the perfect seat to take in the grandeur of the view. Julia settled beside him on the cool stone. The silence stretched between them like an invisible thread, pulling them deeper into the heart of the moment. He slipped off his backpack and pulled out a small bundle of sandwiches, wrapped neatly in cloth. "My grandmother's style," he explained with a smile. "Simple, but perfect."

Julia smiled back, her eyes tracing the horizon. The view was humbling, the kind of beauty that made words feel unnecessary. They sat side by side, sharing the sandwiches in silence, the only sound was the whisper of the wind. Julia glanced at Nicolas, noticing how his expression was calm, almost meditative, he was absorbing the landscape into his very being.

After a long while, Nicolas broke the silence. His voice was quiet. "I know you've always said you don't believe in God, but ... being here, in a place like this, it's hard not to feel ... something. The silence, the vastness of the landscape, and the pristine-ness of nature, it makes me feel there is One beyond this all. Something stirs my mind and heart, as if an ancient memory wakes up in my mind. Like there is Someone higher, an invisible One, who is ever wise and powerful."

Julia turned to him, her gaze soft and thoughtful. His words were not unexpected, but they lingered in her chest like a quiet question. She had spent much of her life relying on logic, on scientific and academic thinking. She thought of the friction between her and her mother who had been always trying to get her to go to church, to read the bible, to praise the Christian understanding of God. How she would always avoid these conversations and hated how she was made to feel guilty and compelled. But now, her understanding and feelings had begun to shift.

She said, "I used to feel that way, that there couldn't be anything beyond what we can see or prove. But ... something changed recently. Since I started going to the Meditation Center, I can't really call myself an atheist anymore. I don't know what to call it, but ... I have felt something deep. Something in the silence. Something beyond the mundane. And maybe I have been wrong all those years."

Nicolas tilted his head, curiosity lighting his features. "What do you mean?"

Julia smiled softly, trying to find words to explain something that had no name. "It's like what I learned about God. I always thought God was something distant, abstract, a concept that you either believed in or not. But now ... I think that God is not a concept. But a living Being. A divine, invisible Being who is endlessly peaceful and makes me feel so still and safe. It's like reconnecting with Someone who loves you unconditionally and who you've always belonged to." She paused, her gaze distant, as if seeing beyond the landscape.

Nicolas nodded slowly, his expression thoughtful. "My Grandma used to say that we can talk to the 'Great Spirit' in silence, in solitude, with no one else between me and the Divine, without any rituals or middlemen. She believed it was about being free from self-interest."

Julia nodded, feeling the emotion in his words. Suddenly it was as if his grandmother was with them, as if her spirit still lingered in this place. "It's beautiful," she said quietly. "What she taught you. It feels... true."

"In the meditation classes they describe God as a Parent, a Being of unconditional love. Someone who sees us as we truly are, beyond all the roles and labels."

Nicolas leaned back, his hands resting on the cool surface of the rock. "She used to say we're all children of the Divine, even the animals, that we should carry that awareness with us. It's not about wealth or status, those things mean nothing to 'Great Spirit.' It's about living with integrity, with respect for ourselves and others. I didn't always understand what she was saying, but her words stayed with me."

Julia's gaze drifted back to the horizon. "That's so beautiful. In the meditation classes they talk about inner security, how it comes from knowing who we really are. They say the 'real you' is timeless, non-physical, untouched by the chaos of life. That we are not the body, but the spirit, the soul. And when you feel that, it's like ... nothing can shake you."

Nicolas was silent for a moment, his eyes tracing the line of the river. "Do you really feel that?" he asked softly.

"Sometimes," Julia admitted. "It's like glimpses, fleeting, but powerful. And at the same time, it's... humbling."

Nicolas nodded slowly, weighing her words. "Grandma used to say the same thing about humility. That when you're truly connected, you stop needing to prove anything."

The wind picked up, carrying the scent of pine and earth. Julia closed her eyes, letting the fragrance and the sounds of nature wash over her. In the back of her mind, she recalled a meditation commentary, words that had stayed with her like an echo. She opened her eyes and looked at Nicolas, her voice tentative but steady.

"Shall we do a meditation? I am learning," she said. "this way to connect, to feel that presence. Can I share it?"

Nicolas turned to her, his expression open, almost boyish in its curiosity. "I'd like that."

Julia closed her eyes for a moment, trying to recall the words that had so deeply resonated with her. She couldn't quite remember all of it. Her lips moved silently, the words dancing on the edge of her mind.

When she opened her eyes again, she looked at him. "I need a moment to remember. It's a guided meditation, how they do it in the course."

Nicolas gave her a small, encouraging smile, and they both returned to the quiet, letting the landscape, the vastness, and the silence weave its way around them once more. Julia closed her eyes, drawing in a steady breath, while she was collecting her thoughts. Her voice was hesitant at first, soft and halting, as though piecing together fragments of Claire's guidance. "Okay … let's start by… making sure your body is comfortable. Just… let your breathing find its own rhythm, soft and steady."

She glanced at Nicolas briefly, and saw him relax while sitting straight. "Now… direct your attention inward. Away from all the external sounds and movements, away from the… the senses. Just let the mind drift into a quiet space inside." Her voice grew steadier as she spoke.

"Beyond … beyond this physical world, beyond sound and change, there is a timeless dimension filled with silence and light. Like a sky beyond the physical sky."

Her pause felt intentional, as though inviting Nicolas to travel with her in his mind.

"A dimension of timeless light and peace. A dimension of still light and eternal belonging. It feels like Home, the Soul world. Home of eternity, Home of eternal peace, Home of eternal belonging. Home of the family of souls and the Supreme Soul.

"No physical boundaries, no limits... just a gentle, endless glow of soft golden-like light and silence. And there... in that stillness... you can start to feel the true self. Not your body, not your name or job or... anything from this world. Just... light, the invisible, imperishable soul. A being of consciousness, like a tiny sparkling star, an immortal experiencer.

"And in that space of silence, of stillness, of endless light," she continued after a few moments of silence, her tone steadier now, "resides the Supreme Soul, the eternal Parent of all souls. The Supreme is a being of light, like... like a radiant star, sparkling and pure. Forever wise, endlessly kind."

The breeze whispered through the trees, carrying the scent of pine. Julia widened her eyes, glancing at Nicolas, who was watching her with quiet attention. Emboldened, she continued.

"This soul, this invisible One, is supremely benevolent and loving. Unaffected by the chaos of the drama of human life or the pulls of this world. The Supreme never forgets the eternal Home or the family of souls. It's... as though this being holds the truth of who we really are."

She faltered for a moment, searching her memory. "The Supreme knows no sorrow, no fear... no anger or arrogance. Just...

purity. No attachments, no desires. It's like... a love so vast, like an ocean. Pure. Free from complications or demands."

Julia hesitated, her voice softening as she added, "You can't see this Supreme One with your eyes. But... you can feel that divine presence, uplifting, comforting. And when your mind connects, when you align your thoughts and feelings with this Supreme Parent, there's this incredible sense of peace. Like... like you're safe in a way you didn't know was possible."

She smiled faintly, her gaze drifting to the horizon. "It's not about being close physically. It's... a silent connection, clean and simple. It's about trust, respect, and knowing you're fully loved."

Nicolas leaned forward slightly, his expression unreadable, but his focus unwavering.

Julia continued with a serene steadiness now. "They say the Supreme offers every relationship. A wise Teacher when you need guidance. A gentle Mother when you need comfort. A protective Father. A loyal Friend. Even... even a loving Companion who is with you in your thoughts and feelings."

Her words lingered in the air like the scent of wildflowers, delicate and present.

"It's... a love that empowers. It's humble, non-imposing but majestic. Uplifting. It's... peace and purity, and the sweetness of being completely understood."

She fell silent, and she carefully looked at Nic, her eyes meeting his. For a long moment, neither of them spoke. The wind played in the treetops, a soft murmur of life moving. Then, Julia smiled shyly.

"That's... how I remember it, anyway," she said, her cheeks coloring slightly. "I'm still figuring it out. But... it's pleasant, isn't it?"

Nicolas inhaled deeply and then exhaled softly, his gaze distant, thoughtful. "Yeah," he said finally. "It is."

They sat there quietly, watching the river thread its way through the gorge, as though the world had stood still to hold space for their quiet meditation.

As they drove back to Hyde Park, Nicolas leaned back in his seat while holding the steering wheel, the rhythm of the car on the road a soft backdrop to his thoughts. The late afternoon sunlight poured through the trees, casting light beams onto the front window. He kept his hands steady on the wheel, his expression calm but thoughtful. Julia also leaned back in her seat, gazing out at the soft blush of the sky. The silence between them was the stillness of two hearts touched by something vast and serene.

He was still mulling over their conversation and the meditation; Julia's words had been hesitant yet sincere, like she was uncovering something fragile and precious. It had surprised him how natural it seemed for her, how she pieced together fragments of what she'd heard, yet infused it with her own quiet earnestness. Her voice had carried a simplicity that drew him in.

He glanced briefly at her. She was gazing out of the window, lost in her own thoughts. Her meditation had stirred in him even more of his grandmother's wisdom, long buried beneath the demands of his life in Manhattan.

Her words came quietly circling back in his mind. *A solitary communion with the unseen, she had called it, a connection beyond words, beyond the physical. You are a son of the Divine, Nic, she would say, her weathered hand resting lightly on his shoulder. Knowledge gives you honor, dignity, and self-respect. Chasing after wealth and comforts happens when one has forgotten their connection with the Creator.*

He thought about his career as a cardiologist at NYU, a life filled with surgeries, pressure, prestige, demands and expectations from patients and the system, hospital routines, and the constant noise of the city. It was a world far removed from the quiet simplicity his grandmother had revered. There was something about the quiet that Julia had invoked that felt nourishing.

It struck him how deeply he missed that sense of inner connection, the silence his grandmother had once taught him. For all his achievements, there was a part of him that longed for that solitude, that communion with the Divine. He thought about her words again, about letting the consciousness of being a son of the Divine infuse every aspect of life. Perhaps that was what was missing, not just in him, but in so many people he encountered. A grounding, a sense of something greater than the endless chase for more.

The serene vibe of the meditation lingered in his mind, like a golden thread tying him back to something essential. He felt a quiet gratitude for her willingness to share, for reminding him of a truth he had forgotten. Maybe, he thought, it's time to find my way back to that silence, to honor the dignity Grandma spoke of, not just in thought, but in living.

CHAPTER 11

A Quiet Evening
and a Dream

The car rolled to a stop in front of her parents' home, its headlights briefly illuminating the garden where her mother's prized rose bushes stood. Julia stepped out, the air cool against her flushed cheeks from the hike and the lingering conversations with Nicolas. He waited until she reached the front door before driving off into the evening, the car's taillights disappearing into the distance.

Her mother greeted her at the door with a mixture of enthusiasm and mild reproach, as was her custom. "You look tired," she said, her eyes scanning Julia's face. "You'll have dinner, won't you? I've made your favorite."

Julia smiled and let herself be drawn into the familiar warmth of home. The table was already set, the scent of her mother's hearty peruvian dishes wafting from the kitchen. Her father sat at the head of the table, flipping through a newspaper with his reading glasses perched on the tip of his nose. He looked up as she entered, his face lighting up.

"Ah, there she is," he said, setting the paper aside. "How was the hike? Did Nicolas show you that secret trail of his?"

Julia nodded, sliding into her chair. "He did. It was... beautiful. The view over the Hudson Gorge was breathtaking."

Her father smiled, his warm, steady presence a comfort as always. "That boy's lucky to have you, you know. And I hope you gave him a run for his money on that trail."

She laughed softly, absorbing the vibes of her family's company. Dinner passed with lighthearted conversation, her father recounting some stories from his firefighter days.

But as the meal wound down, her mother's tone shifted. "Julia," she began, her hands stilling above her plate, "why don't you come to church with me tomorrow? It's been so long. It would mean a lot to me."

The question, usually a source of irritation, now felt softer, less intrusive. Julia met her mother's eyes, seeing the sincerity behind them. "I appreciate the invitation, Mom, but I think I'll pass this time," she said gently. "I really am tired and would like to sleep without alarm and commitment. I'm still processing a lot from the conversations with Nic and... other things. I had thought to take some quiet time tomorrow."

Her mother frowned slightly but nodded, sensing the change in Julia's tone. It wasn't the usual rejection laced with annoyance, but something calm and genuine. "Well," she said, her voice tinged with a mixture of disappointment and understanding, "maybe next time."

Julia leaned over and kissed her mother's cheek. "Maybe next time," she echoed, her words carrying a sincerity that surprised even herself.

After dinner, she excused herself early. She really was tired. The outdoors had worn her out in a pleasant way, and the thought of her soft bed was irresistibly inviting. After a hot shower, she climbed under the covers, the atmosphere of her childhood bedroom enveloped her, and her thoughts drifted toward the day, the grandeur of the Hudson Gorge, the meditation shared with Nic, and the sense of something greater that had woven itself into their time together.

That night, Julia had a dream.

The River of Light

She sees herself standing at the edge of a glowing river, its waters shimmering with golden-orange hues. The river flows silently, carrying tiny stars with a gentle peaceful radiance, like living souls traveling toward a radiant horizon. She felt herself drawn to the river. Stepping closer, her reflection appeared, not as her physical self but as a small, luminous point of light. The river seemed to invite her to join and whispered to her of journeys, of belonging, and of an eternal home far beyond the physical world. She felt light, weightless, and pure.

When she awoke the next morning, the dream lingered, its vividness refusing to fade. She lay still for some time, letting its message seep into her consciousness. Then she rose to greet the day.

The sunlight slid softly through the curtains, filling the room with a warm, pristine atmosphere. Outside, the lawn was still damp with dew, and a few finches hopped from branch to branch on the lilac bush by the window. There was something about a small town morning that made time feel like it had nowhere to be.

Downstairs, the clinking of ceramic cups and the faint scent of toasted bread greeted her. Her mother stood at the stove, softly singing an old Peruvian lullaby that had filled her childhood, one of those melodies that somehow lived in her bones more than in her memory.

"Morning, sweetheart," her mother said without turning, placing a small bowl of scrambled eggs on the table. "Coffee's ready. We've got toast, fruit, and there's a bit of the blueberry jam left if you want."

"Thanks, Mom." Julia poured herself a cup, the steam curling up like incense smoke. She sat down and glanced across the table. Her father, dressed in his faded navy sweater and khakis, was already halfway through his first slice of toast. The Sunday paper lay folded beside his plate, untouched.

Her mother, bustling in her typical pre-church rhythm, dabbed her mouth with a napkin. "I better not be late again or the Hendersons will take my seat." She chuckled lightly, adjusting her earrings. "You sure you won't come?"

Julia shook her head gently. "Not today, Mom."

"Well," her mother sighed, brushing her hands on a kitchen towel, "you two can solve the problems of the world over coffee." With a kiss on Julia's hair and a quick wave to her husband, she was out the door in a breeze of perfume and high heels.

The quiet that followed had a different texture than the one before. It was companionable, like a woolen shawl shared between them.

Her father sipped his coffee, then looked at her thoughtfully. "You slept okay?"

"I slept very well," she said, smiling. "I had this strange but beautiful dream. A river... full of stars. Like living lights floating in light."

He nodded, as though that made perfect sense.

They sat quietly for a few moments, the rhythm of their chewing filling the silence.

"Your mother," he said slowly, "always found her peace in church. She used to take me in the early days. I went to please her. And then, later, for the habit. But I don't know... I never quite found what I was looking for in all that incense and Latin."

Julia looked at him, surprised at the confession. "Why didn't you ever say anything?"

He gave a small shrug, half-smile. "What's the point? People don't always want to listen to why you leave. They just want to know if and when you'll be back."

She nodded, stirred by something quietly aching in his words.

"Your meditation stuff," he said, placing his cup down gently, "what's that like?"

"It's been... unexpected," she admitted, tucking her legs beneath her chair. "I thought it was going to be fluffy or maybe too abstract. But it's not. It's teaching me to step back, and observe more.

He chuckled softly. "So, you are learning to not immediately react or judge before seeing a bigger picture?"

She laughed. "Well, sort of, yeah. It's like... observing the world, letting every scene play out. Just... neutrally observing from that quiet space inside. No ego or anger or tightness."

He nodded slowly, folding his hands on the table. "I've seen a lot of things I couldn't fix," he said. "Fires just burn indiscriminately. And sometimes people burn too, on the inside. All you can do is use your skills, be patient and keep the hose steady."

Julia reached across the table and gently touched his wrist. He studied her, as if seeing her for the first time. Not as his daughter, but as a woman carving her own path. They cleared the table slowly. Outside, the neighborhood stirred, cars starting, a dog barking lazily at a passing squirrel, the wind nudging the leaves like a whisper.

Leaving the dishes for later, they stepped out onto the porch with fresh mugs of coffee, Julia leaned against the railing, her hair caught by the breeze.

"I think I'm learning how to be with myself, and enjoy it," she said softly.

Her father didn't respond right away. He simply looked out toward the hills in the distance, the morning sun casting its golden blessing over their quiet little corner of the world.

"That," he said finally after a deep sigh, "is important. Feeling at ease, … at peace with yourself."

CHAPTER 12

The Echo of Her Voice

Sunlight pooled playfully on the hardwood floor, slipping through the curtains in golden strips that warmed her ankles as she stood barefoot by the bed, folding a sweater she hadn't worn. The quiet of the house was comforting. Downstairs, she could hear the gentle clinking of dishes as her father tidied up the kitchen, humming tunelessly to himself in a way that made her heart ache with tenderness.

The visit had been short, yet it felt as if they had stayed so long. The weekend had unfolded like a series of small doors opening in her mind.

She zipped her bag slowly, the sound slicing gently through the quiet. Soon she'd be at Nicolas' parents for lunch. She looked forward to seeing his mother again, her presence breathed a grace, almost ancestral, that holds both history and wisdom. In her company Julia always felt enriched, in a way that wealth, title or possessions never could.

And then, back to Manhattan. The city that never stopped spinning, where they'd go back to the rhythm and routine of their everyday lives. But something was different this time...

Besides carrying her bag, her mind was carrying a lightness, a quiet excitement, a softness, an eagerness to know more of the subtle secrets that seemed to be infused into life. A willingness to be more silent and observant enough to perceive the unspoken, the invisible. She took one last look around the room. Her childhood books still stood in neat rows on the shelf, the window overlooked the quiet street that had once felt like the edge of the world. And now, it was simply where she came from. A chapter in the story of her journey.

Julia picked up her bag and stepped into the hallway, ready to walk into the rest of her life, a little more prepared than before.

The scent of sage and cinnamon welcomed her as she entered the Van Wyck home, nestled quietly among the trees at the edge of Hyde Park. She recognized the blend instantly. Nicolas' mother always had something warm simmering on the stove, and something quietly soulful lingering in the air.

Nicolas greeted her at the door with a soft smile and took her coat. "She's in the kitchen," he whispered, "making that vegetable stew you love."

Julia followed him through the familiar hallway, past the framed photos of family hikes, school awards, and the two that always caught her eye, a sepia-toned image of a beautiful young Native American woman. And another of Nicolas as a little boy, sitting on a rock with an elderly woman, both gazing out at the Hudson River. His grandmother.

Nicolas and Grandma

Leota White Eagle

Mrs. Van Wyck turned when they entered, a wooden spoon in one hand, her salt-and-pepper colored hair tucked into a braid. "Julia," she said, delighted. "I hope you've come hungry."

"I had a late breakfast with my father, but I will not miss your cooking," Julia replied, her smile blooming with ease.

They settled into the bright, cozy kitchen, sunlight filtering through the sheer curtains, casting dancing patterns on the wooden table. A pot of stew bubbled softly, and a loaf of cornbread rested nearby on a wire rack.

"How was the hike yesterday," Nic's mom said.

As they sat down, Nicolas gently leaned back in his chair, his voice mellow. "We went up the gorge yesterday, to Grandma's trail."

His mother's eyes softened. "You haven't been up there in years."

"I know," he said, glancing at Julia, then back at his mother. "The view was just as beautiful as I remembered it. And we sat there quietly, for a long while. Then Julia did a guided meditation, speaking out loud. She is doing this meditation course."

"You meditated?" his mother asked, pausing to glance at Julia with interest. "Up there on that cliff?"

"Yeah," Nicolas said. "It was unexpected but very nice. It also made me remember... Grandma, and the things she used to say. About the Great Spirit, about dignity and silence... When Julia spoke those meditative words, I just listened... and my mind became so quiet."

Julia looked up, her cheeks pinkening a little. "It just came out. Being in nature, in that place... it just flowed."

His mother nodded. "That place always felt special."

There was a quiet moment where each of them seemed to fall into their own thoughts. Then Julia smiled softly, her hands cupped around a warm mug of herbal tea that Mrs. Van Wyck had just poured. "It's only been two weeks," she began. "There's something about the way meditation works, it's different from anything I've done before."

Nicolas' mother leaned in slightly, curious. "What's it like?"

Julia glanced at Nicolas, who gave her an encouraging nod, then turned back to his mother. "It's called Raja Yoga meditation. It's not about emptying your mind or controlling your breath. It's more like... reminding yourself of something you already know deep down. That you're not just this body or this human personality, but a soul. A spiritual being of light and peace. A traveler, really, just passing through this world."

Mrs. Van Wyck's brow lifted slightly. "A soul," she repeated, thoughtfully.

"Yes. And not just that," Julia continued, "but that there's a dimension beyond. Where all souls come from. Like a home of light and silence beyond matter. And that there's a Supreme Soul too, a kind of spiritual Parent, who's always there. Meditation connects you to that." She paused, a little shy. "I know it might sound strange..."

"No," Mrs. Van Wyck said softly, shaking her head. "It doesn't. Not to me."

Julia exhaled, visibly relieved.

"I used to sit with Grandma," Nic's mother continued, her eyes far away for a moment. "Especially after my father passed. She'd take me out to the edge of the ridge behind our house. We'd sit in silence. No words. Looking out. She used to say the same thing. That we come from a place of light. That we would return there."

"She called it the Great Silence," Mrs. Van Wyck said. "And Great Spirit was not an old man in the sky, but more like a presence. She didn't need rituals. Her faith was quiet... rooted in nature, in solitude and something older than scripture."

Julia sat forward, a kind of quiet wonder lighting her face. Mrs. Van Wyck gave a small smile, her eyes kind. "You know, I've been to many churches and sat through many sermons. But the most peace I ever felt was when I was sitting with my mother on a rock, just quietly.

They were quiet for a moment, the stew simmering behind them, filling the space with warmth and fragrance. Then Nicolas leaned forward, resting his arms on the table.

"She's really into it," he said, his tone both proud and amused.

Julia laughed lightly. "I just started. But... there's something in it that feels true."

Mrs. Van Wyck reached across the table, giving Julia's hand a gentle squeeze. "Then keep going. The world needs more people remembering these things."

And with that, the moment passed into the easy rhythm of lunch. They had steaming bowls of stew, they broke slices of cornbread, and the conversation wandered into recipes, birds at the feeder, and how Nicolas always managed to burn toast when left alone in the kitchen.

Suddenly Mrs. Van Wyck looked at Nicolas with quiet interest. "Anything special that came up when you were meditating?"

Nicolas thought for some moments, "It really reminded me of Grandma, her voice, her stories. That feeling she used to give me, that I was made of something ancient. I realized I don't know much about her. About your side of the family."

His mother leaned back in her chair, folding her hands in her lap. "You want to know?"

Nicolas nodded. Julia watched him, noticing how still he had become. Almost like a boy again, waiting for one of his grandmother's stories.

Mrs. Van Wyck began quietly, her tone gentle, but steady and strong. "My mother was born in the Dakota plains, on reservation land. Her name was Leota White Eagle. She was Lakota, like her father. She believed in silence, in the power of watching more than speaking. She didn't tell me everything. The elders let you learn by observing and thinking things through for yourself. But what she shared... I never forgot."

Julia was listening with full absorption, gently stirring the honey in her tea, the wooden spoon moving in slow circles.

"She used to say," Mrs. Van Wyck continued, "that the soul doesn't belong to the body, but just walks with it, like a guest. And that the earth, the wind, and silence are teachers. She taught me how to be in silence with 'Great Spirit' without asking for things. She said prayer isn't a request, it's a way to realign with 'Great Spirit.' To remember that you are never alone."

Nicolas smiled and seemed to remember something. He ran upstairs and came back with a framed letter. "This is something she had written and given to me a long time ago."

* * *

Pejuta Wíčasa Číkʼala – *Little Medicine Man*

Remember, you are never alone.

The earth beneath your feet is your mother and teacher. Walk gently, for every step leaves a trace on her.

The wind that touches your face carries the voices of your ancestors. Listen, and you will hear their wisdom.

The river teaches you to keep moving, even when rocks try to block your way. Flow around them with patience.

The eagle teaches you to see far, to rise above troubles without losing sight of what is close to your heart.

Be humble, like the grass that bends in the storm yet always rises again.

Be strong, but never forget to be humble and kind. True strength is not in the fist, but in a contented mind and a heart that can forgive.

Speak truth, even when your voice is small. Truth is the bow that never breaks.

And remember, every life is sacred. Respect it, and you will walk in harmony.

* * *

"She must have had that quiet strength," Julia said, when Nic finished reading it. "I can see where you both get it from."

His mother laughed softly, a warm sound. "Grandma didn't believe in controlling others. She believed in mastering the self. Honor doesn't shout," she used to say. "It just keeps walking."

There was a pause, as if the room needed to breathe with that memory.

"She didn't call it religion," Nic's mother said, breaking the silence that had filled the room. "She called it 'the old way. ' She believed that there was a life force flowing through everything. She believed the soul is eternal and travels. Life was seen as a circle, not a line. And you didn't need a temple to find God. You just needed solitude, silence, and purity of heart."

Julia's eyes welled slightly, though she blinked it away. "That's beautiful. In the meditation course, they speak of the soul as a traveler too. A traveler through the world of matter, playing many roles. And at the end of the journey the soul returns to the Home of light and silence."

His mother nodded slowly, the corners of her mouth curling in a faint smile. "My mom used to say that truth doesn't come from outside. It comes back to you." Nic was alertly taking it all in while watching the two women talk.

With an almost comic punctuality the grandfather clock struck 5.

"Well," Nicolas said briskly, rising, "we'd better get going before all this wisdom makes us miss the next train."

They had shared a long lunch and afternoon, stories flowing. Julia felt so content, so comfortable in this house.

CHAPTER 13

The Return Journey

The train eased out of the Poughkeepsie station with a low, humming sigh, the trailing wheels squeaking beneath it as if it was carrying too much weight. Julia and Nicolas sat side by side, the late afternoon sun casting amber light across the compartment.

Neither of them spoke at first. Outside the window, the Hudson River glinted in the fading light, wide and serene, winding its way past trees and distant hills. Everything looked washed in gold.

Julia leaned her head slightly against the window, watching the trees pass in soft blurs. "I always forget how great the view on this ride can be," she murmured, half to herself.

Nicolas glanced at her and smiled. They sat quietly for a while, the silence between them deep and easy. Julia turned to look at him, her voice low. "Your mom... she's incredible. The way she remembers your grandmother, the way she carries that history, not with sadness, but with strength."

Nicolas nodded, his expression thoughtful. "She never tried to push it on me growing up. I think she was waiting for me to ask."

He smiled faintly, gazing out the window. "I used to think of Grandma's stories as… mythology, poetic, but outdated. But lately…" He paused, watching a hawk glide across the sky in the distance. "Lately, it doesn't feel so unreal or outdated."

They sat in that silence for a while longer, the train swaying gently, the daylight beginning to give way to dusk. Nicolas turned toward her, his voice thoughtful. He began, "if you really experience a living relationship with God, I don't think you can ever feel truly lonely."

Julia turned to look at him, curious. "What makes you say that?"

"Grandma used to say that when you really feel that connection, there is no emptiness," he answered.

Julia considered this, her fingers idly tracing patterns on her jeans. "Loneliness is so common, though. It's everywhere," she said softly. "Even people who seem to have everything, families, careers, long-term relationships, they still feel lonely. Like there's this ache inside that doesn't get fixed."

Nicolas nodded. "It's like a kind of 'pain,' an emotional pain, a sadness, isn't it? That feeling of being unseen or misunderstood, even in a room full of people. My patients are like that sometimes, especially the older ones."

Julia let his words sink in, her thoughts drifting to her own moments of alone-ness. "Do you think," she asked after a moment, "that connecting with the Supreme could really change that?"

Nicolas glanced at her, "It's worth exploring," he said. "The way you talked yesterday, about God being so close, like a Parent, a Friend, even a Companion, that sounds... different. Not distant or abstract. Very intimate."

Julia smiled faintly, her expression full of puzzled wonder. "God as a Friend who truly understands you, or as a Mother who nurtures you, even when you don't know how to nurture yourself, she said."

Nicolas nodded, "Not like filling the emptiness with distractions or with people. But it's more about enjoying your own thoughts and feelings and experiencing that subtle company of someone who is ever-wise, ever-loving, and understanding. Someone who is always available and always focusing on the best in you."

Julia turned her gaze back to the window, watching the trees blur into golden streaks. "Experimenting with a clean type of love," she mused. "Not the 'needy' form of love that depends or expects or clings, but a love that's selfless and unconditional."

"That sounds..." Nicolas hesitated, searching for the right word. "Freeing."

"But that is so different from what I felt when going to church with my mom."

They fell into silence again, but this time it was like the quiet before dawn when the world is on the verge of waking.

Nicolas spoke again, his mind spinning with excitement of having found some secret medicine for his patients: "Maybe loneliness is a signal, a reminder, a nudge to look inward, to reconnect to self, to the beyond and to that One."

Julia smiled, her heart warmed by his words.

And as the sky outside darkened into night, a golden thread seemed to stretch quietly between Hyde Park and Manhattan, between past and present. A silent promise, gently unfolding.

CHAPTER 14

The Inner Kingdom

The early evening atmosphere in the room was relaxing and quiet as Julia entered. Outside, the city rushed forward with its usual urgency, but inside the Meditation Center time seemed to loosen its grip. She came earlier because she wanted to sit in the upstairs silence room before the class started. The memories of the experience in that room on her birthday were so vivid and would regularly pull her to go and sit there for a while.

Just before time she came down and settled into her seat, notebook ready, her pen balanced between her fingers.

They began as in the previous sessions with guided meditation. Then Claire stood up at the front with her usual easy tranquility, a marker in hand. She wrote three words in broad letters on the whiteboard:

The Inner Kingdom

Turning around, her gaze rested briefly on each face. "Every soul is a sovereign, a master," she began. "Every one of us has a kingdom to rule. But the question is, how well are we ruling?"

A soft murmur of curiosity stirred in the room. Then Claire wrote the following:

The king (soul), the prime minister and the cabinet

Claire drew the point of light. "The main one in the kingdom is the ruler, the soul. That's you, the invisible experiencer. But a ruler never governs alone. Inside your kingdom there are three ministers working constantly."

She added a rectangle.

"The first is the *mind.* The cabinet of ministers. The mind generates thoughts, images, feelings, emotions, attitudes, vibes, intentions. It is spontaneous, and sometimes restless and unruly. The mind in your kingdom is always producing thoughts and feelings. But if left unchecked, it floods the kingdom with noise."

Julia felt her stomach tighten. *That's me. A thousand thoughts before breakfast.*

Claire drew another rectangle. "The prime minister is the *intellect.* The intellect is the judge. It discerns, decides, and directs. It holds our sense of self, our sense of identity, the bigger picture, our perspective, our wisdom and common sense. The intellect evaluates the activity of the mind and discerns, 'Yes, this thought is useful. No, that one is not. This aligns with truth, this doesn't.' And the intellect decides whether a thought is put into action or not. When the prime minister is wise and strong, he can guide the mind clearly and the kingdom is orderly."

Julia nodded and frowned, recognizing something in that. *Her mind often felt like an unstoppable stream, pulling her in a hundred directions. Cyclical thoughts, worries, what-ifs... she could see how weak her 'judge' had become.*

Claire continued, "The body and the senses are also part of the kingdom of the souls. The intellect allows a thought to be put into action through the body or not. It is also the intellect that evaluates the information that comes in through the senses. It is the intellect that interprets that information and what to do next."

Taking a moment to let it sink in, Claire looked around to see if she had everyone's attention and then went on. "When the intellect is confused, misinformed, or weak, the mind will be influenced by the subconscious and/or the senses of the body. Without the discernment of the intellect, chaos can erupt in the mind."

"And then," Claire continued after drawing a third rectangle, "there is the *subconscious*. This is the treasury of the kingdom. Every experience, every repeated thought, every feeling gets stored there. It holds the impressions, thoughts, and experiences of the past in the form of habits, inclinations, patterns, dependencies, and tendencies. Much of these, we might be unaware that we are carrying. But they influence the mind. The word 'sanskars' is used for the content of the treasury. "

She let the silence hang for a moment. "Now, for example, if your mind is producing negative thoughts, and your intellect is too tired to question them, where do they go? They are brought to expression through the body and its senses and also they go into the treasury (subconscious mind) in the form of a thinking pattern. And once stored, they come back out again, influencing tomorrow's thoughts, tomorrow's reactions. Repetition then makes these stronger; this is how tendencies and habits are formed."

Julia's brow furrowed further. She thought of her own restless mind at night, cyclical thoughts, doubts, insecurities, even silly regrets from years ago. It suddenly made sense: she had been filling her treasury with noise and rubbish.

SOUL/RULER/MASTER

PRIME MINISTER	CABINET (the mind)	TREASURY (the sanskars)
• Discern	• Thoughts	• Impressions
• Decide	• Feelings	• Tendencies
• Perspective	• Attitudes	• Habits
Awareness	• Vibes	

the body /senses

"So how do we rule our kingdom well?" Claire asked, looking around. No one answered but all eyes were towards her, waiting for her answer.

"Through spiritual wisdom and meditation. This strengthens the intellect, the power to discern, to choose. The intellect can then hold a spiritual and broader perspective on self and life and becomes knowledgeable and alert. It can then guide the mind in a constructive way. It can say, 'Not every thought deserves attention.' Only the constructive or virtuous ones should be allowed to be put into action. And then stored in the treasury. Slowly, we can begin to refill the treasury with experiences, impressions, and thought/behavior patterns that are useful or positive or even spiritual. Until the subconscious becomes full of peaceful, loving, and happy sanskars instead of waste, worry, struggle, and sorrow."

Julia raised her hand. "So... the subconscious isn't bad, it's just... like a record keeper?"

"Right," Claire smiled. "And it's loyal, it will faithfully hold whatever you give it. It's up to the ruler, you, to decide what kind of kingdom you want to create. Is it one of confusion and heaviness and deceitful pleasures, or one of clarity, peace, and lasting joy?"

Julia felt a ripple inside her. *I've been letting the ministers run wild,* she admitted silently. *My mind is a chatterbox, my intellect asleep, my treasury filled with clutter. No wonder I sometimes feel so restless.*

Claire put the marker down. "When the intellect holds the awareness that I am a guest in this world, immortal, an innately divine being of peace, the mind can then experience freedom, inner safety, appreciation, and joy, and the kingdom naturally begins to harmonize. When the intellect is clear, the mind becomes calm, the body and its senses can be used constructively, and the subconscious becomes clean. The ruler, the soul, is the master again."

Julia closed her eyes briefly, visualizing the image. A throne, not outside, but within. A calm authority she had forgotten was hers.

When the session ended, Julia lingered, her notebook open, words scribbled half-legible: *Mind, thoughts. Intellect, judge. Subconscious, treasury. I am the ruler.* She smiled faintly, pressing her pen to the page. The stress and insecurities inside seemed less like hopeless burdens she just needed to learn to live with, but more like a kingdom waiting for the king to return.

The group slowly dispersed, a quiet shuffle of chairs pulled softly over the floor, coats slipping on, polite murmurs exchanged. Julia lingered. She wanted to hold the inner peace a little longer, as if afraid it might dissolve once she stepped outside.

When she finally pushed open the glass door, the city rushed back at her in full force, sirens pulsing, impatient car horns, voices rising and overlapping. The familiar but not always friendly restlessness pressed in, but tonight something felt different.

She walked down Fifth Avenue, the words *Mind, Intellect, Subconscious* echoing in her head. Each step was like a quiet experiment.

The mind is working, she told herself, watching her thoughts flicker in and out. *What's it thinking now?*

A sudden memory surfaced, an email she had forgotten to answer. Normally it would spiral into self-reproach, a stream of: *You're behind, you're careless.* But tonight she paused.

Judge it, she reminded herself. *That's the intellect's work.*

She breathed. *Not every thought deserves entry and attention. This one is just noise. I'll answer tomorrow. Let it go.*

The thought faded, like a bubble bursting before it could grow. A surprising quietness followed.

As she crossed 34th Street, she imagined her subconscious, the treasury, like a vast vault. For years she had been filling it with many things, some of it real junk, like complaints, worries, insecurities. *What if I start placing something else in there?* she wondered. *A jewel instead of dust.*

She closed her eyes briefly at the light. *I am peace. I am light.* The words glowed in her mind, delicate yet steady. She pictured herself setting them gently inside her treasury, where they could rest, multiply, return.

When she opened her eyes, the crosswalk signal flashed, and she stepped forward with a small, private smile.

By the time she reached her apartment, the city hadn't changed, but somehow she felt different. She sat by the window overlooking Central Park, notebook open on her lap. Her pen moved slowly across the page:

The mind creates. The intellect discerns and judges. The treasury stores. Through the body and the senses, the part is enacted. And I, am the ruler.

She tapped the words with her fingertip, sealing them in her mind.

She had always felt ruled by her own thoughts, as if they were wild animals dragging her in every direction. But tonight, there was a new image: an inner kingdom and the king returning.

A deep breath escaped her, unforced. She closed her notebook and whispered into the quiet of the room, "I am home."

CHAPTER 15

Karma

The buzz of the conversations among some of the participants faded, while others stopped scrolling and looked up from their phones, as Claire took her place at the front of the room. Julia, settling into her usual chair, felt a quiet anticipation.

Claire's voice, calm and steady, filled the space.

"Let's take a moment to remember..." and she guided them into a meditation on the soul-identity.

"The invisible traveler, the soul," she continued when they had finished the meditation, "is the real self, the being of consciousness moving through time. The soul is visiting this body, using it as a temporary vehicle to interact with this physical realm. But this world is not our true home."

Julia's face showed surprise and curiosity.

"The invisible traveler does not originate here," Claire continued. "The soul is from another dimension, one of light, of silence. A place beyond time, beyond change, beyond matter itself.

This is the eternal Home of souls, and of the Supreme Soul. This is where we come from, where we return, where we truly belong."

Julia closed her eyes, letting the words sink in. A home beyond time. A world of silence and light. Claire's voice had softened into something almost like a lullaby.

Silence settled over the room, deep and still. Julia breathed in slowly.

Not Julia, but a being of light, moving through the currents of time, she thought.

After some moments of silence, Claire stood up and walked to the white board.

"Let's explore one of the most fundamental truths in spirituality: the law of karma." She wrote the word in steady strokes: **KARMA.**

"Many people hear this word and think of fate," Claire said. "Or of punishment. But karma is not about that, nor about superstition or luck. The word 'karma' simply means *action.* And every action, whether a thought, a word, or a deed, has a consequence. It's a law as natural as gravity."

Claire drew a small seed on the board, then an apple tree beside it. "If you plant a seed. What happens?"

A few voices answered, "It grows."

"Yes," Claire nodded. "But more specifically, it grows according to the information in the seed that you planted. If you sow an apple seed, you won't get a banana tree. If you sow anger, you cannot harvest peace. Every action carries its consequences, its fruit. Karma is precise, unfailing."

Julia's pen scratched quickly. She thought of her sleepless nights, her critical thoughts toward herself and others. *I've been planting weeds,* she mused. *And then I wonder why my garden feels overgrown.*

Claire continued, "This is why we say: I am the creator of my destiny. My present is the fruit of my past actions, and my future will be shaped by what I choose today."

"Think of karma," Claire said, "as a subtle accounting system. Every thought, every feeling, every word, every act, nothing is lost. It is recorded in the soul's account. That account comes back to us in the form of situations, relationships, etc., even health. Life is not random, it is a mirror, showing me my own returns."

Julia frowned slightly. Someone in the group raised his hand. "But what about suffering we don't understand? Like someone who's kind, but gets sick. Or a child born into violence or poverty?"

Claire met his gaze warmly. "That's a deep question. The law of karma doesn't begin with the birth of this body, and it doesn't end with the end of this body. The soul carries its ledger across lives. Sometimes we only see one chapter of the story, but the law is unfailing across the whole book. Nothing is arbitrary. Every scene carries meaning, every pain has its message, every comfort has its cause, even if hidden to us now."

A hush spread through the room. Julia felt both sobered and strangely relieved. *So nothing is wasted. Even pain has its reason and is not some random cruelty from the universe. There is a message, a lesson. And every good action will bring its sweet fruit. No matter how hidden or un-noticed the actions may have been.*

Claire uncapped her marker again. "So what is our freedom then? It is the present moment. Right now, I am writing my future. Whatever I have sown in the past and whatever fruits they brought or continue to bring. That is there and let me face it with wisdom and dignity. But now, I can sow a new seed."

She paused, letting the thought settle. "Even if yesterday I planted anger, today I can plant peace. Even if yesterday I planted selfishness, today I can plant benevolence. Every moment is a chance to begin again."

Julia's chest lifted with a breath she didn't realize she was holding. She scribbled the words: *Every moment is a seed. Begin again.*

"Let's practice," Claire said softly. "Try and keep your eyes open. So you can create a meditative state of mind anywhere.

Think of yourself as a gardener. Your mind is the soil, your thoughts are like seeds. What will you plant? Peace? Kindness? Self-respect? Choose, and let the seed drop into the earth of your consciousness. And reflect on the fruits it will bring."

The room fell into silence.

After some time Claire said, "Thoughts, words, actions, attitude, intentions, etc., are all seeds that bring their own fruits." And she quietly closed the session.

Chapter 16

The Eternal Journey of the Soul

The evening at the Meditation Center was calm, wrapped in a soft light that seemed to slow time. The greeting of now familiar faces. The air carried that familiar quiet anticipation before a deep class. Julia settled into her usual seat, notebook in hand. Claire's presence at the front was composed and warm.

"Tonight," she began, "we'll go a little further into the journey of the soul. Beyond this one life, beyond this name and face, into the larger story that has no beginning or end."

The room stilled. Even the faint sound of city traffic outside seemed to pause.

"The soul," Claire continued, "is an eternal traveler moving through time, experiences, and forms. The body is a temporary instrument, a costume the soul wears for a while. Name, gender, nationality, beliefs, even our family, these change over time, but the soul remains. What continues are the impressions we carry: habits, memories, tendencies, and inclinations. The sanskars."

Julia listened, she had not heard much about 'reincarnation' and whatever she had heard she had dismissed.

Claire glanced around the room. "This journey is guided by karma. Every thought, word, and action leaves an imprint on the soul and influences what follows."

A man named Daniel raised his hand. "If that's true," he asked, "why do we see people who harm others still thriving, while those who are kind often struggle?"

Claire smiled faintly. "A fair question. Think of karma as seeds. Some sprout right away, others take time, or even lifetimes, to bear fruit. A person may be enjoying the results of their past goodness while planting something very different in the present. Nothing is lost; it simply unfolds when the conditions are right."

Another participant spoke up. "And what happens when we die? What happens to all that we've accumulated?"

Claire's tone softened. "The soul simply moves on. Death is like changing clothes or switching vehicles. When the body can no longer serve, the soul withdraws, carrying the record of its story, its thoughts, habits, dependencies, vices and virtues. Then, like a traveler choosing a new route, it enters another body. Nothing is erased; it's continuity in a new form."

She paused, letting the idea breathe before continuing. "You may have heard of the research of Dr. Ian Stevenson and Dr. Jim Tucker."[1]

They studied children who recalled details of previous lives with astonishing accuracy, names, places, relationships, all later verified. These studies suggest that consciousness cannot be confined to one lifetime.

In Raja Yoga meditation we understand that certain memories, the tendencies, the personality traits, they travel with the soul."

A woman named Priya lifted her hand. "Is that why some babies are born with fears or talents that can't be explained?"

Claire nodded. "A child's tendencies, their natural likes and dislikes, their bond with certain people, it's shaped by the sanskars carried over from the past. As they grow up, the influences from the present life then further mold the personality. Sometimes you meet someone and feel an instant closeness or resistance. These invisible threads connect beyond time."

Julia thought of Nicolas, how easy it had always been between them, even as teenagers. Perhaps some bonds were simply older than memory.

---

1   Jim B. Tucker, "Ian Stevenson and Cases of the Reincarnation Type," *Journal of Scientific Exploration*, Vol. 22, No. 1, pp. 36-43, 2008.
https://med.virginia.edu/perceptual-studies/our-research/children-who-report-memories-of-previous-lives/?utm_source=chatgpt.com

Daniel frowned slightly. "But isn't it unfair that someone might be born into suffering because of something they don't even remember?"

Claire shook her head gently. "It's not about fairness in a human sense. Karma isn't about blame. It's about signals, messages from life showing where the soul has drifted from its truth and where it's aligned. We may not recall the cause, but we feel the effect. If a consequence or effect is unpleasant or painful, it is an indication for us to change the action that led to that consequence. A simple example, if you put your hand in fire, you will feel pain. You don't blame the fire. You just quickly withdraw your hand. The pain is telling you that you did something un-natural."

All were quiet but you could almost hear the racing of thoughts.

"Sometimes we may have some form of pain or discomfort, physical or emotional or mental. And we are not seeing what is the cause. But there always is. It's up to each one of us to learn to decode the message."

And at the deepest level," Claire continued, "perhaps the message for all problems and ailments is go back to origin. Reposition yourself in this world as a spiritual being. Drop ego and attachment."

Claire continued, "And remember, this journey doesn't end at death. It continues. The state of mind at the final moment has great influence. There's an old saying, 'As are your last thoughts, so will be your destination.' If the soul leaves the body in fear or attachment, those vibrations travel onward. But if one departs in peace, aware of the self and connected with the Supreme, that calm becomes the foundation of the next chapter."

A woman named Lisa spoke softly. "So, our inner state now shapes our next beginning?"

"Yes," Claire said. "Every thought plants a seed for the future. Every reaction, every attitude, is part of the soul's story. That's why awareness is power. Do we act from body consciousness or from soul consciousness."

Eliana, who often sat in the front, leaned forward. "So can we change our karma?"

Claire's eyes brightened. "By changing perspective and awareness. Karma begins in thought, not in the hands. When we return to the soul perspective and hold the awareness of being a soul, light, immortal, virtuous, the quality of our actions changes naturally. Before every decision, ask: *Where is this coming from? Is it from fear, desire, or pride? Or from clarity and compassion?* The source determines the return."

Julia smiled faintly.

"And there is something," Claire added softly. "Remembrance of the Supreme Soul. When the intellect is tuned to the Supreme and the mind experiences the company of the Supreme, love, joy, and stillness fill the soul. It then becomes easy to distinguish between what brings temporary pleasure and maybe even pain over time. And what brings lasting joy and peace. What might promise happiness but can never sustain it. This clarity helps to let go of old habits and patterns."

"The other way that habits may change is through pain and suffering. But that is, of course, not the preferable nor elegant way."

The room grew deeply still.

Claire's voice dropped to a gentle whisper. "Let's take a few moments now to experience ourselves as travelers beyond time."

She guided them into meditation.

Julia closed her eyes even though it had been suggested to try to meditate with open eyes. The space behind her forehead felt bright, as if a small light had been uncovered there. She pictured herself as that light, tiny, steady, aware, moving through the stream of time. Bodies, names, faces came and went, but the consciousness behind them remained untouched, quietly learning, quietly watching.

For the first time, the thought of death didn't frighten her. It felt like walking through a doorway into another morning.

Claire's voice lingered like a calm breeze: "Light… an eternal traveler, a child of the Supreme."

Julia sat very still, a faint smile softening her face. The idea of many lives no longer seemed mysterious or abstract. And in that quiet, she sensed the same truth that had guided her since she first walked into the center, life was much larger than she had ever imagined, and everything in it, somehow, was helping her find the way home.

CHAPTER 17

Karma on the Subway

The subway screeched into the station with its usual mixture of harsh sounds, a piercing metallic wail that had become so familiar. Julia stepped onto the crowded platform, the air thick with morning energy. Commuters jostled each other, earbuds in, coffee cups clutched like lifelines. A man barked into his phone about a delayed shipment, while a mother struggled to calm her toddler, who was clearly unimpressed by the early hour.

Julia found her spot against a pole in the packed compartment as the train lurched forward. The scent of bagels and coffee mingled with the scent of human bodies and the unmistakable tang of the subway. Normally, the noise and crowd might have felt overwhelming, but today, Julia's mind was elsewhere, still immersed in last night's lesson.

The idea of karma as a spiritual bank account had caught her interest. Claire's words echoed in her head: *"Every action is either a deposit or a withdrawal. The quality of your intention is part of the value of the transaction.* "

Julia glanced around the car, taking in the sea of faces. Each one a story, a journey, a soul. She smiled to herself, feeling a sense of kinship with her fellow commuters. "We're all just little points of light," she thought, "traveling through this big, sometimes crazy world. Everyone's trying their best, even if it doesn't always look that way. Thinking of it as a grand theater, then all are invisible actors, playing out a part. The body is their temporary costume."

A man bumped into her, muttering a quick apology before diving back into his phone.

Julia felt a flicker of irritation rise but the thought came: *Deposit peace and calm, Julia. This is your chance to build your karmic wealth.* She responded with a kind smile he didn't see but that lifted her spirit nonetheless.

The idea of karma banking really gave her joy. She thought of the financial world she worked in, the constant calculations, the relentless pursuit of profit. What if she approached her life with the same precision and strategy, but for spiritual gain?

She chuckled quietly as she imagined karma banking as a financial model. *Deposits of virtue, withdrawals of negativity...* she mused. "If I were managing my karmic portfolio, what would my balance sheet look like? Am I operating at a profit, or am I in debt?"

The thought made her giggle softly, earning a curious glance from a fellow passenger. She imagined pitching the concept in the boardroom:

"Ladies and gentlemen, today we're shifting focus from monetary growth to spiritual wealth. Forget the Nasdaq; let's talk karma stock. A smile is worth ten points, patience under stress adds fifty, and gossip? That's a penalty of one hundred."

Her amusement deepened as she thought about her boss, Mr. Benson, raising an eyebrow at the idea. "Julia," he'd say, "I don't think karma dividends are going to impress our investors."

But then again, wasn't there something universal about the principle? Whether in finance or spirituality, the key to growth was the same: make wise, intentional choices.

As the train rattled toward 14th Street, Julia decided on a small, practical goal for the day. *One act of pure, selfless kindness. Something simple, but done with full awareness and love. Maybe helping a colleague, maybe just offering encouragement.*

She closed her eyes briefly, picturing the action as a golden coin being deposited into her karmic account. *I'll start today with one deposit of virtue,* she thought.

The subway screeched to a halt, and Julia stepped onto the platform, her mind clear and her resolve strong. The crisp morning air greeted her as she emerged onto the bustling streets of Downtown. She weaved through the crowds, the rhythm of the city matching her own energized pace.

When she walked into the bank, she greeted everyone with a warm smile. "Good morning, Annie!" she said cheerfully as she passed her colleague's desk.

Annie looked up. "Morning, Julia! You're in a good mood today."

Julia winked. "It's the coffee, and maybe a little spiritual wealth management."

Annie laughed. "Whatever it is, I'll take some of it!"

At her own desk, Julia greeted her boss, Mr. Benson, who was intensely looking at his computer screen. He glanced up briefly, his usual no-nonsense demeanor softening just a fraction. "Morning, Julia. You seem chipper. Big deal in the works?"

"Something like that," she said with a smile. *Big deal indeed,* she thought. *A deposit of peace and joy, right here, right now.*

As Julia settled into her tasks, she kept her resolve at the forefront of her mind. She sent a thoughtful email to a stressed colleague, offered to grab coffee for Annie, and reminded herself to pause and breathe before reacting to any challenges.

Her intention for the day was clear: to manage her karmic account with the same care and precision she brought to financial portfolios. She remembered: *Karma is the wealth of the soul. Each act coming from a more spiritual awareness enriches us, while negativity depletes us.*

And as Julia typed away at her computer, she smiled, she really liked this idea of actions as deposits or withdrawals.

CHAPTER 18

A Dinner Conversation

The glow of the restaurant's soft lighting cast a warm, intimate ambiance over the table where Julia and Annie sat, their plates arranged neatly before them. The murmur of conversations from other diners blended with the gentle clinking of glasses and tableware, creating a comforting background to their evening. It had been a while since the two of them had gone out for dinner together, and tonight, they had chosen a small, charming Mediterranean restaurant tucked away on a quiet street near Central Park.

Julia, browsing the menu, made an effortless decision. "I'll have the roasted vegetable platter with quinoa and tahini dressing," she said, setting the menu down.

Annie, eyeing her with a curious smirk, leaned forward. "Since when did you start eating like a yogi? No steak? No seafood?"

Julia smiled, unfazed. "Since I started thinking more about karma."

Annie arched an eyebrow. "Ah, karma. As if that is the most normal thing in the world," she teased, making a face that had question marks written all over it. She quickly chose a no-meat, mushroom risotto and handed her menu back to the waiter before turning her full attention to Julia.

"Alright, I'm listening. Enlighten me."

Julia picked up her water glass, swirling it slightly before taking a sip. "Are you sure? Do I need to explain my love for vegetables?"

Annie mysteriously and teasingly but in a light and friendly way said, "Tell your secrets. I want to know. Don't preach, but I seriously would like to know what is going on with you."

Slowly Julia started, "It's just that… karma isn't some abstract concept of moral returns. It's actually very practical and also precise. Every thought, every action is like a ripple in a vast lake, shaping what comes next. It's not just about consequence or reward; it's about learning and returning to a state of wisdom and benevolence. And it starts with everyday actions and choices. And diet is one of them."

Annie looked thoughtfully, "Go on. I am sure there is more."

"I love animals," Julia said after a few moments of silent thought. "They are like friends and companions to some extent. They also want to be free and live safely. Why should I eat them, especially when nature is offering us so many other things. The human body can survive and thrive perfectly well on a vegetarian diet."

The waiter approached their table with a warm smile, balancing two plates with practiced ease. "Here we go, … one roasted vegetable quinoa bowl and one mushroom risotto," he announced, carefully setting their dishes down. "Can I get you anything else?"

Julia glanced at the colorful plate in front of her, the aroma of fresh herbs and roasted vegetables rising in the air. "This looks amazing," she said, smiling up at him. "I really appreciate that there are vegetarian options here."

The waiter nodded. "Yeah, a lot more people are going plant-based these days. Good for the planet, good for health, good karma too, right?" He winked playfully before stepping back. "Enjoy your meal!"

Julia chuckled, shaking her head as she picked up her fork. "See? Even the waiter is talking about karma," she said, before glancing at Annie, who was already taking a bite.

"Yeah, yeah," Annie muttered between mouthfuls. "Let's see if karma makes this risotto taste even better."

As Julia reached for a roasted zucchini slice, she glanced at Annie with a thoughtful expression. "You know," she said, "choosing a vegetarian diet is an easy way to create good karma. No creature has to suffer for my meal." She took a sip of water before continuing. "And beyond that, it makes more sense economically and environmentally. Producing grains, lentils, fruits, and vegetables is way less resource-intensive than the bio-industry of meat production. The water consumption alone is staggering, growing plants for food uses a fraction of the water it takes to raise livestock. And then there is the carbon footprint." She smiled lightly, not wanting to overwhelm Annie. "It's a small act of kindness that ripples outward, benefiting not just myself, but society and the planet as well."

Annie rested her chin on her hand. "So, you're telling me the universe is some kind of moral accountant?"

Julia chuckled. "Kind of. Like a bank account. Every action is a deposit or a withdrawal."

Annie leaned back, tapping her fingers on the table. "Okay, but let's be real. Why do some people who do awful things seem to have it all? And why do genuinely good people struggle?"

Julia nodded. "That's, of course, the big question. If karma is fair, why does the bully get the promotion while the honest guy does not?" She paused, choosing her words carefully.

"Maybe this seemingly injustice comes from looking only at the *surface level of life*, limited to one lifetime and the visible dimension. But karma operates on the level of **the soul**, whose journey extends beyond one birth and whose actions are both visible and invisible. Thoughts, feelings, attitudes, intentions are not easily visible on the outside.

"Outcomes do not always align visibly with present behavior. We often see only a small portion of the karmic picture. A person who behaves badly may still enjoy comfort, success, or power because they are spending the credit for earlier good deeds. Another person, pure and kind, may face loss or pain because they are settling the residue of earlier actions.

"Compare it to a tree: the fruit seen now grew from seeds sown long before.

"'Good things' happening to someone who seems 'bad' may reflect: (a) the fruit of earlier good karma, (b) an opportunity in disguise to use that "good" for growth, not just comfort, or (c) the fact that external 'good' doesn't always mean inner good. 'Bad things' happening to someone who seems 'good' may be: (a) results of un-resolved karma from earlier lifetimes, (b) a wake-up call or challenge to deepen awareness, or (c) a reminder that being 'good' in one sense (outward behavior) doesn't guarantee freedom from ignorance, attachment or ego. The question is less 'Why is this happening to them?' and more 'What is *this* saying to me? How can I respond in alignment with my soul nature rather than react from ego?'

"The thing is, karma isn't just about what happens in one lifetime. It stretches across multiple lives. What we're experiencing today is the result of past actions, some from this life, some from another. It's like planting seeds. Some sprout immediately, some take years, even lifetimes."

Annie's eyes narrowed in thought. "So, you're saying suffering isn't random?"

Julia shook her head. "No, it's not. It's a direct result of past choices, sometimes from so far back we don't even remember planting the seeds."

Annie, cutting into her dish, glanced at Julia. "Okay, I think I got that." But after some moments of silence the thoughts were spinning in her head, "But if it's all cause and effect, does that mean we're just stuck in some endless cycle of consequences?"

Julia smiled. "By shifting our perspective, thoughts and actions, we can change the trajectory of what comes next. It's like stepping off the autopilot of old habits and making conscious choices."

Annie took a slow sip of her wine, considering this. "So, if I, let's say, make a habit of snapping at my co-workers, it's not just about the bad day I'm having, it's reinforcing a pattern in me?"

"Right," Julia said.

Annie sighed dramatically. "That sounds like work."

Julia laughed. "It just needs attention. Isn't it good? The idea of being the master of your future," responded Julia equally dramatically.

Annie shook her head in disbelief. "So basically, we all have a karmic rap sheet?"

Julia grinned. "Something like that. But we also have the power to rewrite it. Every moment, every thought, every action is a new entry."

Annie leaned back, exhaling. "That's intense."

Julia nodded. "It is. But also freeing. Because it means nothing is random. We're not victims of fate."

Julia paused for a moment, letting her words settle between them as she took a sip of her tea. The hum of the restaurant, the clinking of glasses and the low murmur of conversations blended into the background. Annie, usually quick to jump in with a quip or a playful remark, was uncharacteristically quiet, her fingers absentmindedly tracing the rim of her glass.

"Karma shaping life experiences, huh?" Annie finally said, her voice softer, more reflective. She twirled her fork in her risotto but didn't take a bite. "Like if you keep making the same choices, you'll end up in the same place, right?" She let out a small, dry chuckle and shook her head. Annie twirled her fork again in her risotto, staring at her plate for a moment before looking up at Julia with a small, reflective smile.

A comfortable silence stretched between them. The restaurant had begun to empty slightly, the murmur of conversations lowering. Julia took a deep breath, feeling light yet anchored, as if the very act of sharing her thoughts and feelings had settled something deeper within her. Annie seemed introspective, but not in a heavy way.

Annie finally broke the silence. "You know what? I think I get it. Karma isn't some cosmic revenge system, it's just about responsibility. Maybe it's about taking ownership of what we think and do."

Annie clinked her glass lightly against Julia's water glass. "Here's to better deposits."

Julia laughed, raising her glass. "And fewer withdrawals."

As they finished their meal and stepped out into the cool Manhattan night, Julia felt a quiet sense of joy.

CHAPTER 19

Walk Across the Brooklyn Bridge

The night was clear, the air cool enough to make their breath faintly visible as Julia and Rachel walked along the wooden planks of the Brooklyn Bridge. Rachel, with her wavy blond hair, still carried that confidence of someone who once lit up every room, but now it seemed covered with a quiet tiredness that Julia just couldn't ignore. The faint rumble of traffic drifted up from below. The river beneath them caught the city lights and tossed them back like scattered jewels. The faint rumble of traffic drifted up from below. The river beneath them caught the city lights and tossed them back like scattered jewels.

They used to do this in college, long walks when exams or love or life felt too heavy to carry. Rachel would talk, Julia would listen, and somehow the world would make sense again by the time they reached the other side. It had been years since one of those walks.

"I swear, Jules," Rachel said, adjusting her scarf against the wind, "I used to love Fridays. Now I'm just exhausted before the weekend even starts."

Julia smiled. "Rough week?"

"When is it not?" Rachel laughed, though it sounded more like a sigh. "Work's insane. Clients losing their minds, my boss thinks that emails at 10 pm are motivational. And Tom..." She trailed off, her gaze slipping toward the skyline. "You know."

Julia nodded gently. "Still feeling disconnected?"

"Disconnected?" Rachel let out a dry laugh. "Try non-existent. We barely talk unless it's about groceries or bills. It's like we're polite roommates who share the rent."

"Have you told him how you feel?"

Rachel exhaled. "I've tried. He listens, nods, promises to do better, but nothing really changes. And I hate sounding like a nag, so I stop bringing it up. Then I get angry, then guilty for being angry. It's exhausting."

Julia listened quietly, her hands tucked into her coat pockets. She'd known Rachel since NYU, bright, ambitious, the kind of person who seemed to live in motion. But now there was a dullness in her eyes, a fatigue that didn't come from work alone.

"I do love him," Rachel went on. "He's not a bad guy. He's just... not there. And I keep wondering if this is just what marriage turns into, all routine, no spark. It feels so empty."

They stopped halfway across the bridge, where the skyline glittered at its brightest. The kind of view that made New York

City feel endless. Julia leaned against the railing, watching the light tremble across the water.

"Can I share something?" she asked.

Rachel smiled faintly. "Something you have been learning in those meditation classes you are going to?"

"Yes, partly."

Rachel laughed under her breath. "Go on then."

Julia looked out at the dark river. "I've been thinking a lot about expectations, how much they control us. We decide how someone should act, and when they don't, we suffer. But what if that need for them to act in a certain way is what's actually making us unhappy, and anxious?"

Rachel frowned slightly. "So what, I'm supposed to stop expecting my husband to care?"

"Not exactly," Julia said. "Just stop needing. When your happiness depends on him being caring and connected, you make yourself vulnerable. You give your strength and peace away."

Rachel tilted her head. "That sounds impossible."

Julia smiled. "It did to me too. But when I started noticing how much energy I put into trying to make people change... and just let that go a little... it felt lighter. I can't control them, but I can stay steady."

Rachel looked unconvinced but curious. "So what, like at work? At home?"

"Well," Julia said, smiling, "take my boss. He loves to micromanage. Before, I'd get so irritated. Now, I just stay calm. I tell myself, 'He's acting from his own stress, not mine.' And weirdly, when I stop reacting, he actually eases up."

"And there is my mother," Julia rolled her eyes. "She often used to push my buttons when she wanted me to do something I don't really want to. Now, I just respectfully decline, staying stable. And it feels so good."

A group of tourists passed by, laughing as one tried to take a photo with the skyline behind her. The bridge moved faintly beneath their feet. Rachel smiled weakly at the sight, then looked back at Julia.

"So if I stay peaceful, Tom will magically start bringing me flowers?"

Julia laughed. "No guarantees. But you might stop feeling miserable waiting for him to."

Rachel sighed, kicking at a loose board. "You make it sound simple."

"It's not," Julia said softly. "But it's liberating."

They walked on, the wind brushing their hair across their faces, the bridge lights throwing long glimmers across the water.

After a while, Rachel said quietly, "You're different, you know," she said at last. "There's something about you lately. You seem lighter."

Julia smiled faintly. "Maybe I'm just learning to let go of what weighs me down."

Rachel nudged her shoulder. "Teach me your ways, oh wise one."

Julia laughed. "One bridge walk at a time, Rach."

Rachel smiled, really smiled, for the first time that evening. The wind tugged gently at their coats as they continued walking, the skyline glowing ahead of them like a quiet promise of something new.

Below them, the river shimmered. A ferry horn echoed faintly through the night. And for a brief, suspended moment, Julia felt it, the simple, steady peace that comes not from having expectations fulfilled, but from stopping the fight with what is.

CHAPTER 20

The Art of Sleeping

The city outside Julia's window buzzed with its usual energy, car horns echoing between the towering buildings. Within the quiet sanctuary of her apartment, she sat curled up on her sofa, a cup of chamomile tea resting between her hands. The dim glow of the lamp cast soft shadows, making the room feel like a cocoon of warmth and solitude.

It had been two nights since she attended the lecture on The Art of Sleeping Well. Apart from the Meditation Course, lectures on all kinds of topics were offered at the Center and she had been curious about this one. Growing up, sleep had always been easy and restful. But for some years now, she struggled with restless nights, some filled with racing thoughts, others with an inexplicable sense of unease. No matter how exhausted she was, the moment she lay in bed, her mind would ignite with activity, replaying conversations, planning for tomorrow, or simply wandering through endless corridors of thought.

Tonight, Nicolas was with her. He had come straight from the hospital, still in his scrubs, exhaustion etched into his face. He had a long day and one patient had passed away earlier that evening. They had spoken briefly about it after he'd showered, but mostly, he had sat in silence, leaning back on the couch, eyes closed, lost in his own thoughts.

Julia observed him, noting the way his breathing had deepened. He would fall asleep soon, just like that. Nicolas had always been that way, able to sleep anywhere, at any time. Now she envied it.

"I don't know how you do that," she said softly, breaking the silence.

His eyes fluttered open. "Do what?"

"Fall asleep so easily. Just… shut down."

Nicolas let out a breath, rubbing his face. "It's a survival mechanism, I think. During med school, I learned to take sleep whenever I could. You learn to ignore everything else and just give in to exhaustion."

Julia looked down at her tea, swirling the liquid gently. "I went to this talk a couple of nights ago. It was about sleep. How we don't just need to rest the body, but also our mind."

Nicolas gave a small smile. "Sounds like something your meditation people would say."

She chuckled. "Well, it makes sense. They said the quality of our sleep is determined by the state of our mind before we go to bed. That if we carry unresolved emotions, stress, or even negative energy from the day, our subconscious keeps working through it, and that's why we wake up feeling tired, even if we slept."

He leaned forward, intrigued now. "And what's their solution? Magic sleep dust?"

Julia smirked. "Close. But no. Detoxing the mind before bed, just like you would brush your teeth before sleeping."

He raised a brow. "I don't see how brushing my brain works."

Julia set her tea down and turned to him. "It's about letting go of the day, mentally reviewing what happened, accepting it, and taking the lessons. They also talked about disconnecting from tv, screens, and work at least an hour before going to bed. And to meditate before going to bed, sort of filling your mind with stillness."

Nicolas considered her words, rubbing the back of his neck. "That actually... makes sense. The way I sleep is more like shutting off a machine, but maybe that's why I sometimes wake up still feeling drained."

Julia smiled, feeling warmth in his openness. "They said that the way we enter sleep sets the tone for the kind of rest we get."

They sat quietly for a moment, both digesting the idea. Nicolas looked over at her, tilting his head slightly. "And? Have you tried it yet?"

She exhaled. "I have. I've started reviewing my day before bed, letting go of any frustrations by finding the lesson for myself in those situations, and then going into meditation. Experiencing the self as living light, an observer of the drama of life, a traveler through time. And honestly… it's helping. My mind doesn't feel as cluttered and heavy at night."

He nodded, thoughtful. "I like that. Reviewing the day, closing it like a book, instead of leaving all the pages open."

Julia smiled. "Yes. Another interesting thing that I have been experimenting with, gratitude. Ending the day with thinking of something I am grateful for. What do I feed my mind before going to sleep? And I wake up lighter."

Nicolas leaned back, stretching. "I think I'll try that. Tonight was… hectic."

Julia reached for his hand, giving it a gentle squeeze.

He looked at her with quiet appreciation. "You've really been absorbing this, haven't you?"

She laughed softly. "It's strange… I never thought this kind of stuff would resonate with me. But it does."

Nicolas watched her for a moment, a tender expression crossing his face. She met his gaze. They sat together in silence. Julia leaned back, letting her body relax, letting go of any unfinished thoughts.

Nicolas had fallen asleep right there on the couch. She gently urged him to go to bed, which he did.

She stayed on the couch and closed her eyes; she allowed herself to surrender to the quiet peace of the night, trusting that sleep would come.

Chapter 21

With Nicolas

Nicolas sat at the kitchen counter, his fingers absently tracing the rim of the coffee cup in front of him. His movements were slow, contemplative. He would stay the weekend. The weight of the week still lingered in his posture even though he slept more than eight hours. He didn't need to say much, Julia could sense it.

She placed a warm cup of fresh tea in front of him taking his coffee cup away, before sitting down across from him. "Rough week?" she asked gently.

Nicolas exhaled, running a hand through his dark hair. "Lost a patient yesterday," he admitted. "Two years. I've been treating him for two years, watching him fight through setbacks, recover, slip again. And yesterday, it just..." He stopped, shaking his head. "We did everything we could. But sometimes, that's not enough."

Julia watched him, feeling the ache in his words. The exhaustion was more than physical, it was in his soul, in the way his eyes held something deeper, something unspoken.

For a moment, they sat in silence, sipping their drinks. Then, with careful thought, Julia said, "I've been thinking and learning about life, death, and what happens to the soul."

Nicolas glanced up, his expression softening into curiosity. "Yeah?" he asked, tilting his head slightly. "What?" he said with eyes that seemed to look for comfort. She hesitated, organizing her thoughts. "In the meditation classes they say that death isn't an end. It's just a transition, like walking through one door into another room. The soul is eternal, and we carry everything, experiences, tendencies, karma accounts, into the next life. Nothing is lost, not really."

Nicolas leaned back in his chair, letting the words settle over him. "You really believe that?"

Julia considered the question. "I don't know if 'believe' is the right word," she said honestly. "But it makes sense. It answers questions I never had answers to before. Like why people are born into such different circumstances, wealth, health, struggles, talents. The idea that we're carrying forward something from a past life... it's strangely comforting."

He nodded slowly, his gaze drifting toward the window. "My grandmother used to talk about things like that," he murmured. "She always told me that the soul is immortal, that we don't belong to this world, not really. Her relationship with God, she called it a 'silent, solitary communion with the Unseen.' That we're sons and daughters of the Divine, and that we should carry ourselves with the dignity of that knowledge."

Julia smiled. "Yes, I remember. You told me on that hike to Angel's Rest and when we talked with your mom. Remember?"

Nicolas sighed, rubbing his temples. "I forget these things as soon as we reach Manhattan."

He was quiet for a minute, "You know, in medicine, we see death clinically. We measure vitals, we track deterioration, we fight it until the very last breath. But we don't really talk about dying what happens after. When a patient dies, we close the file, notify the family, move to the next case. But I've seen it, Julia, moments when someone leaves, when they just... slip away. It's not just the body shutting down. There's something else. Something unseen."

Julia leaned forward, her voice thoughtful. "At the center, they said that the body dies but consciousness transcends the death of the body. The soul travels on with the sanskaras that are there in the soul at that time. And the dying process itself helps the soul to shed ego and attachments. So in a new birth, we can get a relatively clean start. A new body, a new family, a new life can unfold."

Nicolas rested his chin on his hand, absorbing her words.

"Looking at it in that way, dying is not something to dread or resist or to be so afraid of."

Nicolas exhaled, shaking his head. "It's funny. We spend so much time trying to control things, our careers, our relationships, our futures. But if this is true, then we've been shaping our present long before we even got here."

Julia said softly. "At the moment of death, whatever is strongest in our hearts, whatever thoughts dominate, they guide the soul's next journey. That's why being peaceful, being detached, being in the right state of mind matters. Because it carries over."

Nicolas went quiet, thinking of his patient, of the fight, the surrender, the last breath. "And if someone dies afraid? Or angry?" he asked.

Julia sighed. "Then that fear, that anger... it doesn't just disappear. It follows them. It finds expression in the next birth, maybe in the form of anxiety, or restlessness, or struggles they don't understand. And the opposite is true too. If someone dies in peace, if they have no attachments, no unfinished business, then their next birth is light, free, easy."

Nicolas was silent for a long moment. "That's interesting... and powerful if true."

Maybe," he said quietly, "our future is much more in our hands than we realize."

They sat there together, the city stretching out beyond them, the weight of the day giving way to something lighter.

For the first time that evening, Nicolas looked at ease, in peace.

Perhaps death wasn't an end. But a new start.

CHAPTER 22

A Love that Never Leaves

The client was impeccably dressed in a cream silk blouse and camel-colored wool coat, her diamonds subtle but unmistakable, her perfume just strong enough to leave a trail of memory in the air. She entered the bank's private lounge with a kind of practiced grace, but when Julia looked into her eyes, she saw something else, something less rehearsed.

"Julia," the woman said with a tight smile, "I'm not sure why I keep coming here in person when we could just do this online."

Julia offered her the warm, steady presence she had cultivated in these conversations. "Sometimes it's just nice to talk in person. Let's go over the portfolio first."

They did. Julia moved through the numbers efficiently, the client's investments were solid, her retirement plan far ahead of schedule, a million dollar portfolio. On paper, everything looked so good.

But when Julia closed the file, the woman lingered. She stirred her tea twice without taking a sip, and then looked up. "You know," she said, her voice dipping just a touch, "some days I feel like I've built this empire just to have someone to talk to."

Julia didn't say anything at first. Then, gently, "Do your children still live in California?"

The woman nodded. "They're doing well. One's in tech, the other's a documentary filmmaker. I'm happy for them." A pause. "But it's hard not to feel like I've been shelved. Like some old volume they love, but they've outgrown."

Julia hesitated, then said with tenderness, "That sounds… lonely."

The woman's eyes watered, just a little, and she blinked quickly. "Lonely. That's the word I've been avoiding." She gave a small laugh, dry and graceful. "I have assistants, clients, invitations… and still, at night, I sometimes talk to my dog like he's the only one who gets me."

Her eyes lit up when talking about her dog and then the conversation went into small talk about vacations, restaurants, and politics.

Before the woman left, she touched Julia's arm. "You have a calm way about you," she said. "It's rare. Thank you for today."

When she was gone, Julia sat back in her chair, the woman's words echoing in her chest.

Loneliness.

It was a slippery feeling, hard to name, even harder to admit.

As she packed up her things to leave for the day, Julia felt that ache, not quite sadness, but a subtle tenderness toward the world. Toward all the people walking through their own quiet ache. She found herself thinking of something she'd read somewhere.

"Loneliness often creeps in not just from being alone, but from feeling disconnected. This can happen even in a crowd. We want to be seen, we want to feel that we are important to someone at least. And sometimes that need turns into a wound."

That night, back in her apartment, Julia lit a small candle near her window. The city outside pulsed with its usual energy, but her space felt still.

She closed her eyes and let her breathing slow.

Inwardly, she began to shift her attention.

"One can experience the relationship with the Supreme as your closest Friend," she remembered Claire saying once.

Julia let her thoughts go beyond the physical world, into that subtle dimension of silence and light beyond. In her mind, she pictured the Supreme as a gentle, radiant light. Like a living star who has always been there, waiting. Her mind felt so calm, so safe.

"If I turn my attention to the subtle, to the imperishable, to the Home beyond, I can always connect with God and experience that sweet divine company," she thought. "As a loving Parent, a wise Guide… a kind Companion… a silent Beloved.

"And there is also the family of living lights. All are souls. 8+ Billion humans are all spiritual beings, playing out their roles. All are souls, all are children of the Supreme, brothers. An immense family, all imperishable."

And in the warmth of that inner connection, and belonging, something softened inside. Not just the day, but the many layers of emotion, the unspoken fears, the hidden longings. The body-conscious acquired limited identities, all began to melt.

Her mind whispered, without effort. "Safe and loved. A divine Friend who is always available and immortal."

Her mind became immersed in feelings of closeness and connectedness.

Minutes passed like petals falling.

And when Julia opened her eyes, the candle was still burning, the city still alive outside. But inside her, there was quiet. A quiet contentment, a silently blissful feeling of being loved.

Julia remained by the window. Her hands wrapped around a warm mug of herbal tea. The candle's gentle flame flickered in rhythm with her thoughts. Outside, a soft drizzle had begun to fall, misting the glass with beads of rain that blurred the city lights into a watercolor of silver and grey.

She had felt something shift inside her that evening, a tenderness opened by the conversation with her client, a realization that loneliness was a thread that stitched through so many lives. She was lucky, she had found something, someone, beyond even Nicolas or her family. A connection that didn't need words, promises, or expectations to be met. Just her attention. Just her return.

She took one more sip of tea, then slowly walked away from the window and dimmed the lights. The apartment fell into a gentle dusk. Only the candle remained.

She sat down on the floor by her meditation corner. No incense, no background music. Just the stillness. Just the silence.

And in the quiet of her inner world, she whispered the words, not aloud, but gently to herself, from memory, like an echo from some familiar place just beyond time.

"Remembering the perspective from the beyond... the perspective from the Home of Light...

"Focusing on the relationship between the soul... and the Supreme Soul..."

Julia let her mind drift upward again, beyond name, beyond body, beyond humans. She experienced herself as a tiny star of light, subtle and pure, sitting quietly in the center of her forehead. She was not Julia, Nic's girlfriend, the banker, the daughter, but a soul. A being of light.

"The real 'I' is a subtle being... Benevolent and angelic in nature... made of light... child of the King of Light... Who is like an Ocean of Peace and Love..."

"A tiny sparkling star with royal, God-like nature..."

A soft wave of warmth moved through her. Not emotion exactly. Recognition. Like remembering something she had always known but forgotten. Yes... I am that.

"The Supreme is like an eternal Father... a perfect Parent..."

"Ever-wise... unconditionally loving... endlessly generous..."
She felt invisibly accompanied alongside her thoughts.

It was a bit like standing in sunlight with her eyes closed, and still knowing the sun was there.

"A bond between the eternal Father and the child of light... Her mind felt filled with timelessness, acceptance, serenity..."

She felt known and loved, completely. Not judged. Not evaluated. Just... known. Cherished. A love that didn't ask anything, did not try to change or force anything. Just restores the beauty and the dignity of who you always were, underneath the many layers of false acquired identities.

"A timeless bond between the Supreme Father, Mother, and the soul... beyond the senses... beyond ego... a silent love... filled with contentment... pure pride..."

She breathed in slowly. She could almost feel God's invisible smile.

A love filled with respect... a love of belonging... always...

This love was not needy. God never loses sight of His child... and feels that clean love and holds the highest vision, always...

Julia felt something sparkle at the edges of her inner vision, like golden threads weaving through her thoughts.

No need to ask for anything... never any feeling of lacking...

Her chest rose and fell in a natural rhythm. She felt full. Full of something ancient, beautiful, innocent and beyond words.

It's a love that never changes... unconditional and for always, filled with sweetness, elegance, and respect. While at the same time very joyful and playful.

A deep stillness filled the space. Even her breath felt lighter, as though the weight of the day had evaporated into something invisible.

"An always accessible Companion... peaceful and wise... trusting and patient..."

In that joyful quiet, Julia's smile was uninterrupted.

"The heart is completely full... totally content... Whatever is worth attaining... has been attained."

She remained in that state of mind for a while, her thoughts enveloped by stillness and love. The candle's flame flickered a little lower, but the light inside her had grown bright.

When she decided to bring the meditation to a close there was a peace that held her like an embrace.

There was still laundry to fold. And some cleaning to do. But inside, she felt no hurry, no gap. She stood, still carrying that quiet, and went into the kitchen to make herself dinner.

God, she thought softly, as she opened the fridge, *you really are such pleasant company.*

CHAPTER 23

Late Night Call

The scent of warm lentils and cumin still lingered in the kitchen, a quiet reminder of the simple dinner she had prepared after her meditation. Julia had changed into her soft cotton pajamas, the ones with the tiny lavender sprigs printed on them, and curled up under the comforter of her bed.

The apartment was still, but not empty. She felt a kind of gentle Presence with her; she was not alone.

She was reaching to turn off the reading lamp when her phone buzzed on the side table. The screen lit up with Nicolas.

She smiled, thumbed it open, and pressed it to her ear. "Hey," she said softly.

There was a pause, and then his voice came through, low, a little raspy. "Did I wake you?"

"Not yet. I was just settling in."

"I had a feeling," he said. "Something told me you were still up. Couldn't sleep myself."

She wrapped a blanket around her shoulders, sitting up in bed. "You okay?"

He exhaled. "Yeah. Just one of those days. Hectic hospital routine."

"Right," she murmured.

There was a pause. "What about you?" he asked. "How was your evening?"

Julia smiled faintly. "Strangely peaceful. I had a client earlier today, a woman who's... well, lonely, even though she has everything money can buy. And it got me thinking about how many people walk around with that ache. Even in crowds."

Nicolas was quiet for a moment. Then: "O, loneliness... Sometimes patients don't say it, but you can feel it."

"I sometimes feel lonely when you have busy shifts for so many days," Julia admitted, her voice gentle. "But tonight... I don't know. I did this meditation. It was about God and love. Nothing physical though. A love that doesn't expect, doesn't need. Just... is."

They were both quiet for a while.

"My grandmother," he said after a moment, "used to talk like that when she spoke of Great Spirit. That pure kind of love. Not attached to form or object. Just quiet and strong and always there."

Julia closed her eyes, resting her head back. "That's what it felt like."

A long pause. Comfortable.

Then Nicolas said, "You sound different tonight."

"How so?"

"Lighter."

She smiled, eyes still closed. "Not sure what to say. My heart feels warm."

Another pause, and then in a voice so tender it made her heart almost ache, "I'm glad you're finding this."

"I am too," she whispered. "Thanks and hope you have a calm night."

"Sleep well, Jules," he said.

She waited until the line clicked off before setting the phone down beside her. The light was already off. Sleep came to her easily that night, as though her soul had been tucked in by something far beyond the blanket around her shoulders.

That night she slept like a rose. It was still dark when the dream came.

In the quiet hours of early dawn, before the city stirred, Julia found herself walking barefoot on a shoreline made not of sand, but of soft silver dust. The waves enfolding her feet weren't of water, but of light, warm and weightless, shimmering with hues of pearl and pale rose.

The sky above was twilight, scattered with constellations she had never seen, yet somehow felt distantly familiar. And in the midst of it all, there was someone, not a form, but a light, a vibe. A radiant yet silent One who watched her, loved her.

She didn't see Him, but she felt His presence. The supreme Father.

There were no words exchanged, only a stillness filled with recognition.

She stood there, luminous and timeless, as the Ocean of Light gently swirled around her ankles, as though the whole universe was listening, breathing, waiting.

And then, as dreams do, it faded, not with drama, but with a hush. The scene melting into the quiet shadows of her room.

Julia stirred awake.

The morning light was still absent, but the city hummed faintly outside. She turned her head slowly on the pillow and blinked, letting the remnants of the dream settle into her chest like fine gold dust.

She didn't want to lose it.

Quietly, she sat up, reached for the small notebook on her bedside table, the one she had begun to call her "soul journal." She opened to a blank page and let her pen move, almost without thinking, from the center of her heart.

The Invisible Meeting
Feeling the self to be light
Going beyond this gross world of matter
The mind dives into the red-golden light
Into that supreme silence of the eternal Home
Total stillness
A deep sense of belonging
Feeling unpolluted... clean

Totally light
Floating in this infinite, warm red light.
Softly there is the sensing of Your sweet company
Your innocent benevolence... Your absolute fullness
You just seem to know everything
And yet be so quiet

You have everything
Bliss, beauty, love, wisdom,
So totally self-contained
Authentic, uninhibited and unending.
Your presence emanates absolute security
You know eternity and immortality as obvious.

Time fades into eternity

Coming back to the awareness of the body
The world feels so strange, so far away, so gross.

Observing the body, the senses serve
They have no fire in them
They are not intruding

The feelings are angelic, subtle, soft, refined
when the mind is beyond the pull of the body and the
senses.

Your company, and Your vision upon me.
It so totally fills the heart.
It brings unimaginable JOY!

She sat for a while after finishing the last line, her pen resting lightly between her fingers. No emails. No phone. No distractions. Just that quiet aftertaste of eternity.

Then she got up to get ready to go to work.

CHAPTER 24

A New Kind of History

The late afternoon sun angled through Julia's windows, painting slow-moving gold over the walls of her apartment. A mug of herbal tea steamed gently on the table beside her, untouched. Her phone lay face down, silent, and her laptop, open to a blank document, sat waiting for her to type something, anything. But instead of writing emails or to-do lists, Julia found herself gazing out across Central Park, its trees in early fall colors.

There was a strange stillness inside her. The kind that wasn't sleepy or dull, but reflective. She had just finished re-reading the notes from her meditation course, something about this latest lesson had struck her deeper than she expected.

The idea of time as a cycle. Not a straight line that begins in darkness and ends in oblivion. But a wheel. Turning.

For most of her life, she'd shrugged off her mother's talk about Paradise, the Garden of Eden, and original sin. It all felt like a myth layered with guilt, shame, and fear. A story told to keep people in check. But now, for the first time, the idea of a peaceful, perfect world didn't feel like religious folklore. A time, an age, when there was harmony.

She leaned back into the cushions of her sofa and closed her eyes.

The Golden Age. The first era of the world cycle, a time when humanity lives in its highest state of purity, peace, and harmony. A time of natural wisdom, beauty, happiness, and innocence. A civilization of soul-conscious beings. A world without sorrow, conflict, without hunger for power. A time before ego, before even the concept of 'wrong.' Where everyone is naturally soul-aware, aware of immortality, and so naturally fearless and secure.

Nature itself is pristine and abundant, seasons are gentle, the elements are in balance, and the environment supports health and joy.

Relationships are free from ego and based on mutual respect and deep connection.

In this age, there is no need for laws, religion, or punishment. Love and unity are the natural way of life.

It is a time of complete alignment between soul, body, and nature. Paradise.

Julia tried to visualize it. No need for control, because everyone naturally was loving and wise. Each one played the roles they were naturally suited for, based on inner virtue. Leaders ruled not by force, but through purity and benevolence.

She let the image settle. What if... that was true?

What if the Garden of Eden wasn't just a metaphor, but a real epoch in the story of humanity? What if humanity actually began with unity and divinity? The idea warmed her chest.

And then there was the Silver Age, a gentle decline from the golden heights. Harmony still reigned, but it had begun to thin, like the fresh radiance of the morning transitioning into afternoon. The soul was still bright, but slightly dulled. People were still virtuous, but there was still no conflict, no sorrow, but a slow forgetting had begun. The slow shift toward material attraction.

The second era of the world cycle: a time when humanity still lives in peace, beauty, and harmony, but with the first gentle traces of change. Subtly, the idea of 'I' connected with the physical starts to appear in the intellect, but still innocent.

Souls remain pure and virtuous, though slightly less powerful than in the Golden Age, and life continues in joy, health, and abundance.

Nature is still balanced and generous, relationships are loving and respectful, and there is no war, crime, or sorrow.

Arts, culture, and architecture flourish in graceful ways, reflecting the dignity and refinement of the people.

The sparkle is less but spiritual awareness is still natural, and truth and love are still the guiding principle of life.

Julia opened her eyes and stared again out at the city. The honking taxis and cars. The people below scurrying between appointments. All this, the noise, the competition, the division, it suddenly seemed so far removed from that original world.

She thought of how the cycle continued into the Copper Age. The third era, the turning point when humanity begins to lose its original purity and power.

Consciousness became fragmented, and souls started to identify more with the body, roles and objects than with the soul. Paradise was lost and remembered only in stories. Myths. Symbols. Rituals.

With this shift, ego, desire, and attachment slowly grow, bringing the first experiences of conflict and sorrow.

It is in this age that religion emerges, as souls begin searching for the truth they once lived naturally.

Art, science, and culture continue, but moral and spiritual decline quietly sets in, influencing both human character and the natural environment.

The Copper Age is the dawn of duality, light still lingers, but shadows have begun to grow.

And now, the Iron Age, the present. The final era, the time when humanity reaches its lowest state of spiritual power and moral strength.

Body-consciousness dominates, and ego, lust, greed, anger, and attachment shape much of human behavior and is considered natural and normal.

Sorrow, conflict, and inequality become common, and the natural world reflects this decline through imbalance, pollution, and scarcity.

While advances in technology and science are great, they often come without wisdom, leading to both progress and destruction.

Religions, cultures, and ideologies multiply, but unity and truth are often lost in division and misunderstanding.

A time where position and possession is confused with truth and strength, where love is confused with lust and dependency, and where noise smuthers the voice of our conscience.

Yet, Julia didn't feel afraid or discouraged. This was not the end. It is just the darkest night before the dawn, the moment in the cycle that prepares for the renewal during the Confluence Age.

The Confluence/Diamond Age is a short, rare moment in the cycle of time when the old world and the new overlap.

It's the turning point when the past reaches its limit and the future begins to take shape.

In this brief age, the Supreme Soul shares the knowledge to change ourselves at the deepest level, clearing acquired body conscious sanskaras, restoring our original qualities, and building a life of integrity and peace.

Every choice we make now carries extraordinary impact, shaping not just our future, but the world's future.

It's a time to awaken, to realign, and to consciously step into the soul-awake state before the new era begins.

This filled her with hope. With purpose.

A breeze brushed against her window. She got up slowly, tea now lukewarm but still fragrant, and took a sip. In the distance, the sun dipped toward the skyline, casting long shadows across the park.

She didn't feel like a modern woman burdened by the complexities of a broken world. She felt like an actor, a player in a vast drama. A being of light who had forgotten for a while, but was now beginning to remember.

Paradise wasn't lost. It was just forgotten. And it is waiting to be remembered again.

And, she thought, smiling gently, it begins again inside.

CHAPTER 25

The Age We Live In

The next morning Nicolas arrived with a bag of groceries slung over his shoulder, tomatoes, basil, and the kind of sourdough bread only one bakery in the West Village still got right. Julia greeted him with a warm smile, her mind still half-anchored in the thoughts she'd drifted through since she woke.

"Smells like... reflection," he teased, sniffing the air. "Or maybe that's just lavender oil again?"

Julia laughed and shook her head, setting the kettle on the stove.

"I couldn't stop thinking about that lesson on the cycle of time," she said, half to herself, half to him, her eyes staring at some invisible point in front of her. "Especially the Golden and Silver Ages. It sounds so real and possible. Like... maybe we really did start from something beautiful. And maybe the whole human story is just us gradually forgetting who we are."

Nicolas raised an eyebrow, unzipping the bag. "You're talking about the world drama, right? The five ages. What you shared the other day of your last meditation lesson? "The paradise eras? With perfect health and zero taxes?"

"Right, those," she said, sliding onto a stool by the counter. "But not like fantasy. More like a memory, like something deeply buried but somehow familiar." She paused, watching the steam curl from the kettle's spout. "When I was little, my mom used to tell me about the Garden of Eden. But I always thought of it as just some poetic metaphor. A fairy tale. Now, I don't feel like that."

He stopped slicing the bread, looking at her thoughtfully. "So what do you think happened? If that kind of peace really existed... why did it end?"

Julia folded her arms, leaning into the warmth of the kitchen. "That's what's so interesting. They say it didn't end with a single act of disobedience, but more like a slow forgetting. A gradual loss of self-awareness. The soul forgets being a soul and starts identifying with the body... and from there, it's an ongoing decline."

"Sounds a lot like what Grandma used to say," Nicolas murmured. "That the spirit got tired... distracted by all the noise."

Julia nodded. "Instead of experiencing the happiness of soul-consciousness, we started to get attracted by temporary things. Creating desires, expectations, chasing stuff. And it's not like anyone's to blame, it's just the nature of the cycle. It's how energy runs down over time. Everything new becomes old."

He was silent for a moment, slicing with more care now, more thought. "I've been thinking about what you had shared about that lesson on time being cyclical and those different eras. And honestly, it is a very refreshing model of life and human history and it makes sense. It explains many things."

Julia turned toward him, curious. "Like what?"

He paused for a moment, his gaze distant. "Like the hospital. The world in general. The chaos we're living in. I see it every day, patients suffering from preventable things, people numbing themselves with whatever they can find... alcohol, pills, sex, distractions. Doctors burning out. Nurses breaking down. The system is cracked, and everyone's trying to hold it together with tape."

He glanced at her. "If this is the Iron Age, the age of further decline. It's not so much a punishment but more a result of a lack of understanding about deeper laws and truths. As if we have been unconscious and just operating from ego. And as a result, increasing negative karmic accounts which manifest in discomfort, problems and misery on all levels. But in this spiritual model of the cycle it is just a sign of the time. And it is time for a reset."

Julia's eyes softened. "You really have been thinking about these things too, I see. What struck me most is that there's no need to judge or despair. It's just... the night part of the cycle. The phase before dawn."

"Still," Nicolas said, taking a sip of his glass of orange juice. "It's hard sometimes. Seeing how much people suffer. I used to ask myself why. Why would a God allow this kind of pain? I saw kids die during COVID, Julia. Grandparents alone in ICUs.

Families watching loved ones fade through glass or they could not even get to hospitals."

He looked down, then added quietly, "But this idea, that it's a cycle, and that souls are on their own journeys, and that all will return to the soul world, it offers something the textbooks never did. Not easy answers, maybe, but a kind of... perspective. Which makes more sense than anything else I have heard so far."

Julia nodded slowly, "I know what you mean. I used to think humanity was evolving, progressing. But lately I've started wondering. Yes, there is more wealth and technological advancement in certain ways, but there is more conflict than ever at all levels in people's lives. There is no contentment, peace, or joy that lasts. No health, no inner wealth."

"And," Nicolas said, "it appears that so many are totally disconnected from themselves, from each other, and from something higher."

"The Iron Age," Julia murmured. "The age of death. Of confusion. Of mistrust and egotism. Of craving and noise. Of short-lived pleasures and excitements. Arrogance, lust, and greed rule human behavior. The tail end of the story. The time when everything has become chaotic and broken, when systems don't work, relationships are strained, and humanity has forgotten who they really are, who they belong to, and from where they have come."

"But," he added, eyes meeting hers, "if it's a cycle... it starts again, doesn't it? There is a reset, a return to the beginning?"

"The Confluence Age," she said. "It's when the Supreme returns, to restore wisdom and higher consciousness. It's the time of reawakening. Of the soul turning inward again."

Nicolas was quiet for a while. "It is so funny yet interesting that it was my unplanned birthday gift to you." He was remembering the night of her surprise birthday party.

She looked at him, smiling, her eyes sparkling. "Best birthday gift ever."

He laughed softly and then he was silent for a moment. "So are we at the threshold of the Confluence now?"

Julia thought for a while and then slowly said, "I guess so... yes."

CHAPTER 26

The Light Between Them

The kettle had started whistling and at first they did not seem to notice. It gradually grew persistent and Nicolas reached over and turned off the stove without saying a word. The sound faded, replaced by the soft hum of city life just beyond the windows, the muted siren in the distance, the faint rattle of steam pipes in the walls. But inside, everything felt still.

Julia stood up, her hand gently pulling him by his arm. "Come," she said softly, leaving the half-cut bread on the counter and leading him to the corner of the living room where her small meditation space had slowly taken form. A low table, a white candle, a simple tray with a few river stones and on the wall an image of a point of light surrounded by a golden, red, orange glow. She had received that poster as a gift from the Meditation Center and had framed it. She used it to focus her gaze on when she meditated. The afternoon sun filtered through gauzy curtains, casting its light across the floor.

They sat, cross-legged, on floor cushions.

Julia lowered her eyelids almost automatically, but she had now trained herself not to close the eyes and she exhaled, her voice barely more than a breath. "Let's just be quiet for a moment…"

Nicolas followed her lead.

"In the center of the forehead," she began gently, "resides the real 'I'. That's the being of consciousness. The soul. Just a tiny point of living light."

She paused, holding the silence for a few moments.

"The real self is not this body, not the roles I play, not even the thoughts that come and go. The real self is the one who uses the eyes to see… who uses the ears to listen… The invisible experiencer. A guest in the body, a guest in this world, a traveler through time."

Nicolas sat with eyes closed. His mind became so quiet and light. Her words were like invitations.

"Stepping back from the forces and movements of the physical world, the attention is shifted to the subtle and the still and the imperishable beyond. Try and come back to that awareness of self as light, an immortal and free spirit," she continued. "A state where we are naturally full of peace, innocence, absolutely secure, joyful, and playful. A being without needs or confusion.

"Beyond this world of matter is the eternal Home, a world of stillness and red-golden-like light. In the Home, and in that state of mind, there is the presence of the Supreme. A Being of light, of kindness. The Ocean of wisdom and peace. A feeling of being enveloped in silence and love washes over the mind."

Julia fell quiet for a while, she was obviously lost in the experience.

"And from that eternal Home, that gentle light, the soul, pure and virtuous, travels into the dimension of matter and incarnates in a body. A perfect, complete human in the Golden Age. That was the beginning of a cycle of time."

Her voice slowed again, her mind was immersed in the experience.

"A harmonious human world. No fear. No sorrow. No ego. Just peace and total comfort. Human minds without desires, no expectations, no ego. There was inner fullness and so there was no need to prove anything, no rush, no noise... only benevolence and dignity. A world where human beings are naturally soul-conscious."

She let that thought rest in the air, and the room seemed to soften even more.

Nicolas felt a warmth behind his eyes, not tears, but a kind of melting. His grandmother's words, the ones he used to brush off as mystic poetry, began to resurface. "The soul meets the Great Spirit in solitude, with a sincere mind free from arrogance and greed."

She used to say that when they sat together by the lake at dawn, wrapped in quiet. Back then, he didn't understand what she meant. But now, he felt it.

She used to describe silence as, "not just the absence of sound, but an inner stillness, a state where nothing is disturbed, or out of balance. Not empty but full. A state where thoughts are quiet, naturally calm."

Nicolas' mind became immersed in a deep calm.

His grandmother's voice came back. "Train your body to be strong and still, not stiff but at ease, no tension, no rushing, not pushed to act by lust or arrogance.

"One should be like a candle's flame in still air – unmoving, yet full of light and fully present. Like a tree rooted deep, swaying yet unshaken – steady amidst all winds. With a dignified, graceful, self-controlled, and self-confident manner.

"Be at ease with yourself, always. Have a clean and clear conscience, always."

Julia was silent and her body was still. A kind of sweet and almost angelic vibe emanated.

In this silence, the city felt impossibly far away, like a vague memory in the shadow...

Nicolas could feel his breath moving in waves, soft and slow. There was no need to speak, no need to move or to touch. Just be.

And in that stillness came another memory, his grandmother's stories of the Great Spirit. She had described that Being as living, ungraspable, yet personal. It had always remained very vague for Nicolas.

But here Julia spoke of God as 'Father of the soul,' pure and radiant, giving without asking, silent yet always near.

His mind drifted further, resting in the invisible thread between the soul she described and the values his grandmother lived by. A kind of natural nobility, she'd called it once, where a person lived not for gain or glory but for truth, courage, for upliftment of others and kindness. Where character mattered and your words were sacred. Where generosity was the highest honor. Where respect for life, every human, animal, tree, bird and the earth itself, was not philosophy but instinct.

Somehow, it all made sense now. Julia's Golden Age.

His heart softened further. He didn't feel like he was meditating. He felt like he was remembering.

They both sat there silently, breathing, Julia's eyes were open but Nic had closed his, as if suspended in some light-filled space outside of time.

Then slowly, after what felt like both a minute and a lifetime, Julia broke the silence. "You felt it, didn't you?"

Nicolas nodded, not needing to say anything more.

They rose, not in a rush.

They looked at each other with silent understanding, with respect.

"Lunch?" he asked. She smiled. "Let's not forget the bread."

Julia walked barefoot into the kitchen, her fingers absently reaching for the kettle again. The earlier stillness hadn't left; it had just followed her, softening the air around her movements.

But somehow, neither of them felt like coming into sound. They both sat down again with just a mug of tea.

After a while, Nicolas broke the silence. He was still filled with the memories of his grandmother.

"Juul, my grandmother used to try to show me the importance of silence and solitude."

He paused a few moments, trying to recall and even visualize the childhood scenes with her again.

"It's when body, mind, and spirit are in harmony, when there is absolute self-control, that a human being becomes truly noble, truly aware."

Julia listened to him with full attention. "Being a master over the self," she said and they both fell silent again.

After some time Nicolas again broke the silence but this time he wanted to shift into a different mode. He was hungry.

"Okay," he said with mock seriousness, "What's the plan for this mysterious lunch you promised me?"

She smiled and pulled open the fridge. "We have cheese, stuffed tomatoes from last night, a very sleepy avocado, and the sourdough bread that you had started to slice earlier, tomatoes and basil that you brought this morning."

Nicolas leaned on the counter, arms crossed. "That sounds like a poem disguised as a sandwich."

He continued slicing the bread while she mashed the avocado, their movements easy, rhythmic. The sunlight spilled across the counter, pooling between the mugs and the spice jars. A few pigeons shuffled along the windowsill, peeking in like curious neighbors.

"So," Nicolas said after some time, "I talked to my mom last night. She's already planning the tree."

Julia raised an eyebrow. "It's not even December."

He shrugged. "Remember, in her calendar, Christmas begins in November."

Julia chuckled, spreading the avocado with a fork. "And your dad?"

"He's flying back from Lisbon on Friday," Nicolas said. "He wants to do the lights this year. Again."

"Which means you and I will be untangling them for half a day."

"Exactly."

They both grinned.

"Have you told your mom yet we'll be staying in Hyde Park for two full weeks around Christmas time?" Nicolas asked, handing her the tomatoes. "Coming weekend I'm on duty but we can go next weekend to help decorate and in December we will be there for about 14 days."

"Not yet," Julia said. "I think she'll be thrilled… and also use it as leverage to get me to go to Christmas Mass."

Nicolas raised an amused brow.

"She means well," Julia added. "And this year… maybe I'll go. Not because I'm converted. But because… I don't feel like resisting anymore. I feel like honoring her."

He nodded. "It's crazy. But I keep remembering my grandmother so much, since you started this meditation thing. She used to say that peace means learning to listen, even if you don't agree."

They stood together for a while, assembling the sandwiches in comfortable silence. The reflective atmosphere of the morning, its stillness, had woven itself into the buttering of bread, the slicing of cheese, the planning of holiday lights and traditions.

As Julia reached for the kettle once more to steep the chamomile blend Nicolas had brought, she looked up and smiled.

"Isn't it beautiful," she said, "how something as simple as making lunch feels… so nice? Like we didn't leave the meditation at all."

Nicolas nodded, reaching for two plates. "That's the real yoga, isn't it? Tranquility in motion. Peace in the middle of a sandwich."

They laughed and clinked their mugs in a toast, the feeling of moments undisturbed.

CHAPTER 27

Stillness in the Park

By late morning, the city had opened its eyes. Crisp sunlight danced between the late autumn branches of Central Park, casting shadows along the winding paths. Julia, wrapped in a soft charcoal coat and her favorite deep green scarf, walked slowly beneath the elms, her breath forming soft clouds in the cold.

There was no destination in her mind, only the gentle pull to be outdoors and among trees, to walk and to breathe.

Last night's dream still shimmered faintly inside her, like a warm glow behind her ribs. The poem she had written sat quietly folded in her coat pocket, though she had no intention of sharing it with anyone. It was hers, something private and tender, a reminder of the nearness of the One she was beginning to call her Friend.

Birdsongs wove between the branches above, and the city's background noise faded as she walked deeper into the park. The world felt momentarily suspended. Quiet. Clear.

She passed a bench where a woman sat hunched forward, her coat open despite the chill, a stroller in front of her with a sleeping toddler inside. The woman's face was pale, her gaze heavy on the gravel path as though watching something invisible.

Julia had almost walked past, but something, a quiet nudge from inside, made her pause. She turned slightly, and their eyes met.

The woman blinked, startled, then looked away quickly.

But Julia offered a small, gentle smile and said, "Cold morning."

The woman gave a weary chuckle. "Yes. Cold and long."

Julia hesitated only a moment. "May I sit for a bit?"

The woman nodded, clearly surprised. "Sure."

They sat in silence for a few minutes, watching a young boy across the path chasing pigeons while his father looked on.

The woman sighed. "Some days feel like they'll never end. He," she motioned toward the stroller, "hasn't slept properly in three nights. And I haven't had a real conversation in... I don't know. Weeks?"

Julia glanced at the sleeping child. "He's beautiful."

A soft smile crept onto the woman's lips. "He is. Just... It's hard. His dad works overseas. I've got no family here. It's just me. Me and him."

Julia nodded slowly, feeling the subtle ache behind the words.

"Sometimes," she said gently, not with pity but with empathy "we don't realize how much we're carrying until someone asks us how we really are."

The woman looked at her again, eyes searching. "And what if no one ever asks?"

There was a beat of silence.

Julia inhaled softly. "I've been learning to find strength in silence. Not the lonely kind, but the kind that… connects me with something higher."

The woman tilted her head. "Like religion?"

"Not exactly," Julia said, smiling and extremely surprised by herself. Making conversation with a stranger? And that also about something personal? But something pushed her to go on. And the woman seemed eager for her to go on. "More like a friendship. Or the Divine. Or whatever name you like to use for God. I've been learning that it's possible to feel not so alone, even when no one else is around, because there's this… Supreme One. Who doesn't judge. Who doesn't need me to be perfect. Who is just always there, lovingly."

The woman didn't respond right away. She stared at the sleeping child, her expression softening. "That sounds… really nice."

They sat together a while longer. A warm breeze passed like a whisper, unexpected for November, brushing an orange-red colored leaf into Julia's lap.

She looked down at it and smiled. "You know," she said, picking up the leaf and handing it to the woman, "sometimes we don't need answers. Just reminders. That we're seen. And held."

The woman turned the leaf in her hands, her eyes misty. "Thank you," she said softly, "you have no idea how much this means to me."

Julia stood slowly, touched the woman's shoulder gently, and offered a last kind smile. "You're not alone. And also you have your beautiful child."

As she continued her walk, she felt gratitude. And maybe, it had taken root in someone else too.

CHAPTER 28

A Glowing Stranger

They sat across from each other at their usual cafe in SoHo. It was a cold, wet evening, and the windows were fogged with the breath of a dozen half-finished conversations. Annie had insisted they meet. She'd texted. "We need coffee. Real, non-zen coffee."

Julia smiled as Annie arrived, dripping rain and sarcasm in equal measure. Her long coat was open, her curls frizzed out like an electric halo.

"I brought sugar and sass," Annie announced, sliding into the seat opposite Julia. "You brought... chamomile?"

Julia raised her teacup in mock salute. "Mint, actually."

Annie narrowed her eyes. "You've changed."

Julia laughed. "Have I?"

"Oh, definitely," Annie said, unwrapping a croissant and tearing it dramatically in half. "You meditate now. You don't eat steak. You leave parties before the music gets good. And you drink mint tea." She squinted. "Are you even Julia Callaghan anymore?"

Julia rested her cheek in her palm, smiling. "I'm still me. Just… maybe a bit more observant."

Annie leaned forward, elbows on the table, voice softening. "Don't get me wrong, I love that you're glowing. But are you sure this isn't just a phase? A spiritual sugar rush?"

Julia chuckled. "Honestly? I've asked myself that too. But it feels true and stable. It feels like I am remembering something that was always in me. And if it turns out to be just a phase, that is fine too."

That made Annie pause. She tilted her head, chewing slowly. "Remembering what?"

"I'm not sure," Julia said, "certain values. It's not like I've had some huge revelation. But I like the meditation and I am making more conscious choices."

Annie watched her for a moment, her usual quick wit folded into thoughtfulness. "You sound like someone in love."

Julia looked up, surprised.

"But with what or with who?" Annie asked mischievously, smiling. "You and Nic have been together forever. Or are you 'renewed in love'?"

Julia smiled faintly. "In love?… With silence, maybe. Or with who I am when I'm quiet."

Annie groaned, grabbing her chest. "Oh no. You've gone full zen now… I knew this would happen the moment you stopped ordering lattes and wine."

Annie reached for her coffee, then paused with the cup just below her lips. "And how's Nicolas taking all this? The meditating, the vegetables, the philosophical answers?" She raised an eyebrow. "He used to joke that you were the most practical woman he knew. Now you're sitting cross legged in silence and are writing journals," Annie smirked with a tinge of sarcasm.

Julia smiled into her cup, the steam curling toward her like a secret.

"He likes it. We sometimes meditate together. It also makes him feel good and calm."

Annie raised an eyebrow. "He meditates too? Nicolas?"

Julia nodded. "Yeah, sometimes. I think it's making him remember things he'd buried under years of hospital corridors and city living. His grandmother used to teach him about Native American wisdom. He told me that. About how she believed in the power of the invisible, the quiet. What I'm discovering now... is not completely new or strange to him. She used to sit with him by the river and teach him to be silent."

Annie stirred her coffee slowly, lips pursed. "Okay, that's... kind of beautiful. But also kind of intense. Like, are you two becoming one of those couples who chant mantras and burn incense at brunch?"

Julia laughed. "No incense. And no mantras, I promise. But it's good. For both of us, I think. We're having new conversations. Real ones."

Annie picked at the edge of her napkin. "Look, I'm not trying to drag you back to tequila nights and rooftop parties. I just..." She looked at her. "You were always the rational one. The one who helped me make spreadsheets for breakups and plan six months ahead like a pro. Now you talk like you've wandered out of a cloud. That's not necessarily bad. Just... different."

Julia nodded, serious now. "It's not that I'm a completely different person now. I still have deadlines. I still check my bank balance twice a day. But I'm not afraid to be still anymore. I don't need noise to feel alive."

Annie looked down. "Sometimes I wonder if you're leaving us behind. Me. The old Julia."

"I'm not," Julia said quickly. "But I am leaving behind my stress, insecurities and useless thoughts. I was always running. Even when I looked calm, my mind was sprinting laps around itself."

A moment of quiet passed between them. The rain outside had slowed to a mist.

Julia added softly, "You're one of the few people who I'm really close with. That hasn't changed."

Annie nodded. "Okay. But if you start talking about wearing white robes and renouncing chocolate, I'm staging an intervention."

"I would never renounce chocolate," Julia grinned.

"Good. Then I'll allow the mint tea."

They both laughed, the kind of laughter that made the other tables glance over with faint smiles. But under the surface, Julia sensed the question wasn't going away. Not from Annie. And not from inside herself.

Was this a phase? A temporary high?

She didn't know. But, not knowing didn't feel like weakness.

They sat a while longer, sipping slowly, the old rhythm between them not lost, just gently rearranged.

CHAPTER 29

The Enemy Within

The Meditation Center was quieter than usual that Wednesday evening. Outside, New York moved in its usual rhythm, traffic lights blinking through fogged windows, footsteps and city sounds filtering through layers of glass.

Julia settled into her usual spot in the classroom, her notebook in her lap, pen already uncapped. Claire stood at the front, not yet speaking, just looking at everyone with that usual calm, reflective expression.

"Tonight's lesson is a bit of a paradox," she said. "Meditation is about peace. Yet the deeper you go into silence, the more you start to realize… you're on a battlefield."

Julia blinked. *A battlefield?*

Claire smiled gently, acknowledging the reaction. "That's right. Not out there," she gestured vaguely toward the world outside, "but in here." Her finger tapping at her temple. "The inner battlefield. And if there's a battlefield, we must understand the enemy."

She let the words hang for a moment before continuing. "There are two main forces that keep the soul from experiencing true peace: Ego and Maya.

1) Ego. The false identities we carry in our subconscious and which express in different forms but create an undercurrent of insecurity. And it can manifest in anger, lust, greed, dependencies, competition, etc.

2) Maya. Our limited understandings, confused/distorted beliefs, and illusionary ideas."

Julia felt some excitement with this new insight. She thought of how much she'd clung to being competent, liked, and productive. The praise at work. The subtle pride in saying she didn't 'need religion.' Ego. She saw it now.

Maya is what pulls us into body-consciousness. Into temptation, resistance, distraction, self-sabotage. It whispers things like: 'Do it later.' 'It's not that bad.' 'You're too tired today.' Maya will even dress up like logic and convenience.

The group chuckled quietly in recognition.

"And when you begin to meditate sincerely, that's when Maya starts resisting the most. Not because you're failing, but because you're actually progressing."

A woman raised her hand. "So Maya... is like our inner saboteur?"

"Right," Claire said. "But it can be very subtle. It can come disguised as something reasonable. A comforting thought. A familiar excuse. Even a noble justification. You'll know it by its fruits, anything that eventually leads you away from your peace, your clarity, your truth."

Julia took notes quickly, but part of her was just listening. Absorbing. Recognizing.

Claire shared an example of a smoker who wants to quit, how the desire to stop is immediately met with a flood of rationalizations: "You've tried before." "It's not that bad." "Everyone needs a vice. Even non-smokers also get sick and die." That was Maya's voice.

"You need to see it from a distance," Claire said. "Create space between the 'real you' and these thoughts. Don't argue. Just observe. Then bring in a higher thought. Bring in wisdom, that is the antidote."

She paused, letting the group catch up.

Someone else asked, "But what if I know it's Maya and I still fall for it?"

Claire smiled knowingly. "Then you've just learned something about how she operates. That's still progress. Every time you recognize her, you weaken her influence. Don't be discouraged. Be consistent. That's where victory lies. Increase your understanding. The joy and the wonder experienced in the soul-awake state, in meditation, will weaken Maya. And Maya will even start to look silly."

Julia sat with that. A kind of courage stirred in her. Maya wasn't some evil thing to be feared. But a manifestation of some level of ignorance to outgrow. With clarity. With practice. With love for the higher self.

As the lesson closed, Claire reminded them, "You're not alone in this battle. Many are on the same journey, reclaiming their truth. And God, the Supreme, sees you not as broken, but as brave. The Supreme holds the vision of your victorious form."

The group sat in meditation. Julia closed her eyes and inhaled slowly and reflected on the inner kingdom, the battle, and the victory. And the supreme Guide.

CHAPTER 30

Cracks in the Mirror

It started with a croissant.

Flaky, buttery, and warm, the kind Julia used to buy from the little French bakery on 85th before she began her experiments with vegetarianism and self-discipline. She hadn't even planned to eat it. But it was a busy Thursday morning, and she'd rushed out of her apartment without breakfast. A client had brought a box into the office as a treat, and there it sat, aromatic, innocent, practically glowing in its paper wrapping. Her stomach growled. She knew the croissant had eggs in it, which were not part of her new vegetarian experiments. Her mind whispered, "Just this once."

Before she knew it, it was gone, and with it, a quiet sense of inner stability.

The guilt didn't come from the pastry. Not really. It was deeper, a disappointment that she had given in so easily. That she had let the sweet tempting voice of Maya talk her into letting go of her aim. She could hear the whisper again: "You're being too hard on yourself. It's just food. You have enough on your plate already, no need to be so extreme."

This whole week had been heavier than most. Maybe it was the cold November drizzle that seemed to settle in her bones, or the monotony of small irritations at work, the client who complained over nothing, the emails that multiplied like flies, and the faint pressure of self-doubt and now a slight guilt had added.

All day long, that same voice continued its soft campaign: "You're tired. Why meditate tonight? You can skip just this once."

As she left work tired, with a heavy mood, Nicolas texted that he had to take over the weekend shift from a colleague so she would probably not see him until Sunday. She had initially promised herself a nice evening experimenting with a new vegetarian recipe. She'd bought groceries earlier in the week, kale, cherry tomatoes, a block of tofu she wasn't entirely sure how to use, but as she walked home past her favorite Peruvian café, the scent of roasted chicken and garlic pulled her back toward memory.

She hesitated outside the door.

It was only a dish. Lomo Saltado (a popular Peruvian stir-fry dish that combines marinated beef with vegetables and is typically served with French fries or rice). Her childhood comfort food. Her mother used to make it on Sunday nights when the house smelled of cumin and fried potatoes and the radio played old Spanish ballads. What would one night matter?

Inside, the warmth of the restaurant wrapped around her. She placed the order, almost by instinct, and sat down by the window.

When the food arrived, her hands trembled just a little. "Maya is really playing with me these days," she thought. But she took a bite anyway.

At first, it was everything her body remembered, familiar, rich, satisfying. But by the third bite, her stomach felt unsettled. Not from the food. From somewhere deeper. As though she'd betrayed something fragile inside her. A small whisper of integrity was trying to counteract Maya's voice. Something about being true to your principles and respecting yourself.

She pushed the plate away. "I'm sorry," she murmured under her breath, unsure who she was speaking to.

As Julia sat and closed her eyes, she felt a weight still lingering in her chest. The doubt from before had come back knocking more loudly now.

That night, Julia sat in her room, she knew something had shifted. Not catastrophically, but subtly. It wasn't about the croissant. Or the Lomo Saltado. It was the sense that she was slipping quietly back into her old self.

"I'm fooling myself," she thought. "One moment I'm talking about higher consciousness and peaceful vibes... the next I'm giving in to a craving like a tired child."

She tried to focus, to return to the golden silence she had tasted before. But nothing came. Just doubt.

"I'm too busy. I deserve a break. I'll meditate tomorrow. This world is too hard for spiritual ideals."

The candle flickered, casting long shadows against the white wall. The room felt too quiet. Almost accusing.

She wanted to get up. To distract herself. To scroll. To clean. To open a bottle of wine.

But instead, she stayed, and continued to focus on her meditation.

She remembered the session from a few days ago, but it felt more real now: that ego and Maya don't attack with weapons, they seduce. They come dressed as comfort, convenience, and logic. Ego builds the case. Maya argues it for you.

She saw it now.

"Sometimes we stumble," she remembered Claire saying, "and feel we've failed. But in truth, each stumble is just another doorway. What matters most is not that you fall, but whether you choose to get up."

She took a deep breath and whispered, "Not tonight, Maya."

She listened to a guided meditation and then started to write in her journal. Talking to Maya and talking to God.

Then she sat quietly, spine straight, and turned inward, not with the strength of triumph, but with the humility of beginning again.

Not proud, not fully resolved. She realized that progress wasn't always a straight line.

CHAPTER 31

Real Victory
is Silent

It was raining.

Not dramatically, just a steady drizzle that made the sidewalks shine and umbrellas bloom along Fifth Avenue. Julia walked without one, hoodie pulled up, the collar of her coat tight around her neck. Her bag was light; she had left the journal, the water bottle, even her headphones behind. She had nothing to hide behind today.

She had just come from a brunch where an old friend had made a few lighthearted jabs about her 'monk life.' "Still doing that no-meat, early bedtime thing? You must be fun at parties. Poor Nicolas. Is he also not allowed to eat meat and drink alcohol anymore?" Julia had smiled. Laughed. Even nodded. But inside, it stung more than she thought it would.

It wasn't the joke, it was the echo of Maya's favorite line: "If you continue like this, you won't fit in anymore."

By the time she reached her apartment, soaked through and cold, she was tired. Not just physically, but soul-tired. She collapsed onto her couch, still dripping, and stared at the ceiling.

"Why am I doing this?"

It wasn't a dramatic cry. But it was a questioning bordering on doubt.

Something she'd heard in the course came to her mind, "The journey will not simply be, having perfect meditations or following the purest diet. It is also about building up strength. And for that, tests will come. To see how sure you are. How clear you are. And when you sometimes fall down quietly in private... and still choose to rise, again and again, with love for yourself, that is how real power increases."

And slowly, like dawn pressing against the edge of a long night, a new thought emerged, not from outside, but from within. A quiet, crystalline thought: *Why am I doing this? Because I've tasted something real.*

"Real peace. A kind of self-respect that didn't depend on compliments or validation."

She remembered the metaphor used in a class: "Wise fish are not fooled by the bait." And she had seen the bait clearly that day, approval, inclusion, an easier road.

But she also remembered something else. The antidote.

She closed her eyes. In her mind, she shifted her attention to the invisible and timeless self, innately divine, a living light, free and safe. An eternal child of the Supreme. No judgment. Just pure regard.

In that inner quiet, the 'need to be acknowledged, to be respected' dissolved. Not into bitterness, but into clarity.

This, she thought, is real power.

She got up, changed into dry clothes, made herself a cup of herbal tea, and sat at her window watching the rain. No need to prove anything to anyone. She wasn't starting over.

She was beginning deeper.

The next morning, she walked through Central Park in the early light. The leaves were brittle underfoot, golden and brown, and the branches swayed as if whispering some old, forgotten story. And for the first time in days, she felt okay again.

Not because she was perfect, but because she had fallen, and was still choosing to stand again. Taller and wiser.

CHAPTER 32

The Lights on the Tree

The late November air in Hyde Park carried a quiet kind of joy, the hush that came before snow, the early twilight casting colors against the bare trees, and the smell of chimney smoke curling from rooftops. Julia and Nicolas arrived just in time for what had become a family tradition in both their homes: the setting up of the Christmas tree, a full month ahead of Christmas.

Their first stop was at Nicolas's parents' house. The familiar rhythm of the home greeted them, the way the stairs creaked near the top, the scent of pinecones and cinnamon wafting through the hallway, and the warm embrace of Nicolas's mother.

Boxes of ornaments were already waiting in the living room, along with strands of twinkling lights and garlands fluffed and ready. The tree itself stood tall and proud near the window, its fresh needles filling the room with their gentle fragrance. His father, who wanted to help with the lights and had initially set his mind on being with them, was unexpectedly away on a transatlantic flight, so this year the trio worked together, laughing over tangled wires and dusty ornaments.

As Nicolas crouched beside the tree, fiddling with the first strand of lights, his mother unwrapped a delicate glass angel from a nest of tissue paper. She held it up to the light, smiling softly at its silver wings before glancing over at her son.

"So," she said casually, as she hooked the ornament onto a low branch, "how is it at the hospital these days?"

Nicolas looked up, half-grinning, half-sighing. "Busy," he said. "Always busy. Three patients discharged last week, two new cases the next morning. It never really stops."

Mrs. Van Wyck gave a knowing hum. "I imagine not. But you still love it?"

"I do," he said, sitting back on his heels. "Even when it's hard. It's not the hours that get to me, it's the losses. The unpredictability of it. You can do everything right, and still…"

He didn't finish the sentence. Julia, nearby, gently shook a silver garland loose from its twist and didn't say anything. She knew that pause in his voice.

Mrs. Van Wyck came to sit on the arm of the couch, the box of ornaments now forgotten beside her. "I think your grandmother would've said that's the hardest part of service," she said, "is when the heart stays open even after being broken a few times." She used to tell me that pain, when carried with dignity, makes you wise. That there's strength in staying human, even when the world tries to harden you."

Julia looked up then, her fingers gently brushing against a small, hand-painted globe ornament. "That sounds like something she'd say."

"She'd say it often," Mrs. Van Wyck said with a soft chuckle. "Especially when I came home complaining about school or friends. She'd just nod and say, 'Yes, child, the world will bruise you. But don't ever stop being kind.'"

There was a silence, the kind that rests among people who understand each other.

Then Nicolas reached for the next string of lights, threading it carefully through the branches. "I try, Ma. Some days... I wonder if I'm making a difference. But other days, I feel like I'm exactly where I'm supposed to be."

She looked at him with that tenderly motherly glance, "Sometimes your kind presence is all that is needed."

Julia glanced at him, their eyes meeting for a moment. She saw the tiredness behind his smile, but also the quiet strength he carried like a steady current beneath the surface. The tree, half-lit now, seemed to glow a little more.

Mrs. Van Wyck stood up, brushing pine needles from her skirt. "All right, you two," she said with mock sternness, "less philosophizing, more decorating. This tree won't dress itself."

But even as they turned back to the ornaments, a thoughtful stillness lingered in the room.

And Julia's thoughts were pulled to a celebration at the Center. She brushed a pine needle off her sleeve, and felt to share.

"At the Meditation Center," she began, "we had a holiday event. There was a talk about the Christmas tree... not just as a decoration, but as a symbol. They called it the Tree of Humanity."

Nicolas's mother looked up. "The Tree of Humanity?"

"It's a metaphor," Julia explained, her voice thoughtful. "The seed is God... the Supreme. The trunk is the original, unified humanity, when things were pure and in harmony, what they call the Golden and Silver Ages. Then over time, as souls became more body-conscious, different branches emerged: religions, ideologies, systems. Each one had its flowers, like saints, prophets, sacred texts. Even the arts and sciences are branches. The whole tree is beautiful, even though some parts are older, some newer."

"And the Christmas tree?" Nicolas asked, sitting down on the couch as she spoke.

"It's like a memorial," Julia said. "We decorate it with lights, just like the souls, the points of light on the Tree of Humanity. We celebrate it during winter, at the darkest time of the year, almost as if we're remembering light and life when everything around us seems asleep. It really moved me."

Nicolas's mother had stopped hanging ornaments. She sat on the edge of a nearby chair, her hands resting on her lap.

"That is interesting," she said softly. "The symbolism of trees has always been part of the old ways too. In our culture, trees are living elders. You talk to them with respect. The earth, the sky, the elements, everything is part of a living family. Even Christianity, in its pure form, carries that, this idea of light coming into the world, of renewal and forgiveness."

Julia felt a warmth in her chest, not from the fireplace, but from the atmosphere in the room.

"I always thought," Nicolas's mother continued, "that the tree in our living room wasn't just for show. It reminded me of the stories passed down from my mother. The way she spoke of time as circular. Life and death as seasons. Everything part of a great dance."

They all fell quiet again, content to hang the final ornaments without hurry, without fuss. It was a special kind of silence, filled with a warmth that didn't need words.

Chapter 33

Christmas Decorations

The Sunday morning at Julia's parents' home began with the smell of cinnamon rolls and her mother humming Christmas carols in the kitchen. The whole house felt dressed for the season already, garlands on the staircase, golden candle holders lined on the windowsills, and a wreath with red berries hung proudly on the front door. Yet the living room stood waiting, its tall pine tree braced in a corner, half-dressed in lights, surrounded by boxes of carefully packed ornaments labeled in her mother's neat handwriting.

Outside, the streets were quiet, the kind of quiet only small towns can offer on a Sunday late November, crisp, gentle, without hurry. It reminded Julia of how time used to move when she was a child, measured not by hours but by family traditions.

Julia and her father were just finishing breakfast with a cup of hot chocolate when the doorbell rang. Nicolas arrived midmorning and Julia's father greeted him with a familiar warm grin. "Just in time," he said. "Julia's mom has been waiting for someone to climb the ladder."

Her mother emerged from the kitchen, wiping her hands on a red-checkered towel. "That star isn't going to put itself up," she said, raising her eyebrows at Julia before offering Nicolas a genuine smile.

The mood was cheerful as they unwrapped delicate angels, tiny wooden figurines from Peru, a porcelain nativity scene, and strands of twinkling lights. Nicolas helped Julia's father with the ladder and the high ornaments while Julia took charge of the middle branches. Her mother, true to form, directed the decorating with quiet authority, though her tone was more playful than usual.

As they worked, the conversation shifted naturally toward the deeper meanings of the season. It was Nicolas who opened the door this time.

"You know," he said, placing a glass snowflake near the top of the tree, "yesterday, when we were decorating at my parents' house, we ended up having this conversation about what the tree really symbolizes."

Julia's mother paused, her hand stilling over a ribbon. "Oh?"

"Yeah," Julia chimed in gently. "At the Meditation Center, we had a holiday celebration for this season of lights. They shared their understanding of the Christmas tree. That it symbolizes the Tree of Humanity. And it made me think differently about Christmas… about how so many traditions are tied together in one tree."

Her mother raised an eyebrow, but didn't interrupt. Julia took it as permission to continue.

"I mean… Christmas is the celebration of the birth of Christ, right?" she said, holding a soft velvet ornament in her hand. "It's the beginning of Christianity, a new branch emerging on the Tree of Humanity. A whole new religion was born."

Her father tilted his head thoughtfully. "A Tree of Humanity? With different branches, representing religions?"

"Yeah," Julia nodded, encouraged. "So they explained it, the trunk of the tree represents the early time in human history when everything was in harmony, everyone was pure and peaceful. Over time, as humans started to forget their spiritual identity, different religions emerged as branches. Like Judaism, Buddhism, Christianity, Islam… each one a response to the longing to return to that original state, to that harmony. The decorations on the tree symbolize the prophets, the saints and those who play a special role within the specific branches, and the gifts they bring, teachings, scriptures, institutions, etc. And all the lights are a memorial that humans are actually souls. Living lights. And the light at the top of the tree is a memorial of the Supreme Soul, God."

Julia's mother was still now, her hands folded, the ribbon forgotten in her lap. "So you're saying… all religions are part of the same tree?"

Julia met her gaze with warmth. "That's what I'm beginning to understand. That each religion emerged to give people some guidance. All are part of the unfolding of the Tree of Humanity."

Her father smiled faintly. "Like a family. Everyone's got their place, their timing. Their role. Their importance."

Her mother looked unconvinced, but something had softened in her face. "I don't know. It's just... we were taught that Christianity is the only path."

Julia nodded, her voice gentle. "I feel that the metaphor of a tree for humanity is very beautiful. Christianity is a big branch. Christ's message of love, forgiveness, humility, it's timeless. Seeing and appreciating the whole tree doesn't diminish the importance and beauty of the individual branches."

There was silence, but not an awkward one. A silence of consideration.

Her mother looked down at the nativity set they had just placed under the tree, touching the small figure of the baby Jesus. "I suppose," she said slowly, "People can try in different ways to be good. Search in different ways to find answers."

Julia smiled and quietly placed a golden star somewhere on the tree.

They continued decorating in an atmosphere that was both lighthearted and respectful. Stories flowed, her mother shared memories of Christmases when Julia was small, Nicolas told them how his grandmother used to weave Native American stories into the Christian tales she learned later in life.

They all asked him to tell one of those stories. Nicolas leaned back, smiling faintly as if the memory itself carried the smell of sage and woodsmoke.

"My grandmother used to tell the story of 'The Two Fires' when I was little," he began. "She said it came from her people, but that she'd learned to braid it together with the stories she heard later, in church."

He paused, his tone softening, almost reverent. "She'd say that in the beginning, before there were names for things, the Great Spirit breathed into the world two fires. One was the Fire of Light, gentle, warm, golden as dawn. The other was the Fire of Desire, bright, restless, red as sunset. The first fire burned to give, the second burned to have.

"In the beginning only the Fire of Light lived in human hearts. But as the ages passed, the Fire of Desire made its way into their hearts and gradually grew and began to burn wild and hungry. It whispered: *"Take, and you will be more."* And the Fire of Light grew dim beneath the smoke. Then one day, the Great Spirit came to walk among the people, but they did not see Him. Their eyes were clouded.

So He sent them a special child, one of light, born to remind the world of its forgotten fire.

He did not speak of punishment or fear. He spoke of remembrance.

He said: 'The kingdom of heaven is the Fire of Light that burns quietly inside you. You were never meant to lose it. You were meant to tend it.'

"And my grandmother would look at me and say, 'When you feed the right fire, the world becomes spring again.' Then she'd pinch my ear and laugh, 'And that's what prayer and kindness really are, tending your Fire of Light before the Fire of Desire burns everything down to smoke.'"

Nicolas smiled again, softly this time. "I didn't realize then how deep it was. I just liked the image of two fires in the heart. Now... I am beginning to grasp the deeper meaning."

The last ornament to go up was the star for the top.

Julia's mother handed it to her quietly. "You put it up."

Julia climbed the small stepstool, the star in her hands glistering in the afternoon light. She placed it carefully atop the tree, adjusting it until it stood straight, luminous.

Below her, Nicolas and her parents stood together, looking up.

The tree stood there, twinkling with quiet dignity, green and full and beautifully decorated, with many lights.

Julia looked at it and thought: a beautiful representation of the genealogical tree of the human world family.

Later, Julia and Elena went into the kitchen with the dishes.

Elena gestured her to come close and while she was drying the dishes she said softly, "Mija, I noticed you've been... quieter lately. Reflective. You used to say you didn't believe in anything beyond what you could touch."

Julia looked at her with warmth in her eyes, "I still don't fully know what I believe. But I am open to explore, to listen. And meditation really does something with me."

Elena: "I can see that. And you never were like this before. You would always resist going to church. You're beginning to listen, maybe?"

Julia didn't answer. She shrugged, but a small smile tugs at the corner of her mouth.

Elena continued gently, "Just don't be afraid to trust your heart. Sooner or later we will all find our way home."

CHAPTER 34

At the Hospital

The hospital never really slept.

It breathed, pulsed, churned, through code blues, early rounds, and the late-night flicker of hallway lights. Even on a mild Tuesday in December, the hum of monitors, muffled footsteps, and low conversations wove a relentless, however familiar, rhythm through the cardiology wing at NYU Langone.

Nicolas moved through it with a calm precision and a quiet competence he had cultivated over the years, white coat pocket heavy with notes and pager, stethoscope bouncing lightly against his chest, his name badge swinging slightly with each stride.

It was barely past 8 a.m., and Dr. Nicolas Van Wyck was already deep into the day's rhythm as he entered Room 312, where an elderly woman lay propped against white pillows, her hands folded delicately over the thin blanket.

"Good morning, Mrs. Parnell," he greeted gently, checking her chart. "How's the heart treating you today?"

She smiled. "Still beating. That's something, right?"

He chuckled softly, examining her vitals. He joked with her that laughter makes the heart strong so she should continue smiling. Moments like this made the job feel tender and deeply human.

His fifth patient went almost 20 minutes over his planned time, an elderly man who just needed someone to listen, more than anything. And even as he'd nodded with a friendly smile and eyes focused, a familiar anxiety was buzzing at the edges of his mind. The clock kept ticking. A resident waited outside the door to review two new patients he had seen. Down the hall, another patient was prepped for a stent.

Nicolas moved from one task to the next with practiced grace, but internally, the tug of something deeper, something calmer, persisted.

It had been a long year, and a long few years before that. Ever since the pandemic struck just months into his first full year as an attending, life had never really returned to what it once was. The scenes from the early days still hovered like faded polaroids in the back of his mind: the intubated patients, the exhausted nurses, the solemn silence of goodbyes whispered through eyes only, behind layers of PPE. Sometimes it came back to him in flash impressions, a look, a sound, the smell of hand sanitizer. Sometimes it returned as a tug at his chest when the day slowed down and the elevator climbed floors in silence.

Lunchtime was a welcome moment in his day where he could briefly catch his breath and quickly debrief with colleagues while eating and typing his notes. Actually it was more like inhaling lunch then really sitting down to eat. He found a seat in the physicians' lounge with his usual crew, Tomás from pulmonary, Ravi from endocrinology, and Jonah, the surgical fellow who was not yet thirty and already looked like he hadn't slept in a year.

"I swear," Jonah said, unwrapping a protein bar, "I blinked and it's already Wednesday. I forgot what sunlight looks like."

Tomás raised a brow. "We all did. This place eats weeks."

"Or years," Ravi added. "Sometimes I think we live here more than anywhere else."

Nicolas sipped from his thermos of ginger tea, watching the light filter through the window blinds. "You ever think about slowing down?" he asked, almost to himself.

Jonah scoffed. "Slowing down? What's that?"

"No, seriously," Nicolas pressed. "I mean… just getting out. Nature. Silence. Breathing. I've been thinking about it lately."

The others nodded, their expressions suddenly more subdued.

"I used to go hiking upstate when I was younger," Nicolas said, almost wistfully. "There was a spot near the gorge. My Grandma and I used to go there. We'd sit for hours, not talk, just listen to the wind in the trees. It's strange, but I feel more like myself when I'm out there."

Tomás tapped his coffee mug. "You're lucky you remember what stillness feels like."

Ravi sighed. "Maybe we all need a bit more of that."

Two others joined them at the table: Leo, a vascular surgeon with a sarcastic sense of humor, and Samir, a warm-hearted internist who had recently become a father.

"You ever think," Samir said, sipping a lukewarm coffee, "that we're just spinning on a treadmill that someone forgot to switch off?"

Nicolas smirked. "Only every other day."

Leo chuckled. "Speak for yourself. I'm running on fumes and denial."

They all laughed, but it wasn't hollow. It was the kind of laughter that carried an undercurrent of truth, shared among those who had walked through fire and kept going.

Then Samir leaned back and glanced toward Nicolas. "You've been different since a couple of weeks, man. You still enjoy the job, but... I don't know, you've become quieter. Even when things go south, you don't flinch like you used to."

Nicolas considered that. "I have been thinking lately more and more about how we always try to fix everything the way we're trained to," he said. "We're so focused on what's visible, measurable, and treatable. But during those early months of the pandemic... all we had were our eyes, our hearts. Sometimes, all you could offer a patient was your calm presence. And sometimes that felt like enough."

Leo raised his glass of juice in a half-toast. "Philosopher-doctor over here."

The conversation drifted to weekend plans, none of which included rest. Someone mentioned drinks downtown tonight, but even though he would usually go with them, this time Nicolas politely declined. "You guys go. I'll pass. Think I'll just grab some fresh juice and maybe walk a bit. Need to clear my head."

Later that evening, he did just that. In a juice bar in Hoboken, he ordered a fresh large orange juice and stepped back onto the sidewalk. The air was cool and crisp. The chaos of the hospital and the city felt far away.

There was a part of him that longed for stillness. Not just a quiet evening, but a life paced with meaning, surrounded by trees and trails, not just echoing hallways and endless patient charts. He thought of his grandmother again, her old stories about the dignity of all life, her reverence for silence, her belief that all things have a spirit. He could still hear her voice: "Walk with respect, Nic. Even the wind listens."

The first snow of the season started to fall. Each flake drifting gently downward, like a pause written across the sky. It was strange, snow hardly came in December in the city or in this part of Jersey. But, it did today.

He'd never considered leaving medicine, not really, but he did wonder if there was a way to live differently. Less fragmented. Medicine could be his gift to society, but it didn't have to be his entire identity.

Julia's voice floated back into his mind, her words quiet yet deeply anchoring: "You're not just a doctor, Nic. You're a soul. A being of peace."

He sipped his juice and nodded slightly to himself. There really was a kind of change in him. Maybe it was time to plan another hike. Or finally take that long weekend in the woods somewhere. Maybe it was time to learn how to pause again, regularly.

His grandmother had once said, "We weren't meant to live in buildings all day. You've got to let the wind pass through you sometimes."

As he walked on the Waterfront, juice in hand, he paused and looked up at the stars faintly visible above, and across the river was the Manhattan skyline with a billion lights.

He closed his eyes for a moment.

Just breathe. Just be.

The snowfall had turned heavier now, blanketing the side-walk in quiet white.

Nicolas reached for his phone. He turned it over in his hand, staring at the screen for a moment. Then, with a slight smile, he opened a message to Julia.

Nic:
It's snowing in the city. And here in Jersey too.
Strange how the world looks softer when it's covered in white.
I was thinking of that river dream you once told me.
When are you free for another hike into the quiet?

He hesitated for just a moment, then added:

Nic:
Sometimes I wonder if the world's trying to whisper something.

I think I've just started learning how to listen.

He hit send, then slipped the phone back into his pocket.

Julia was sitting by the window in her apartment, legs curled beneath her, a half-read book resting against her chest. The city below moved in slow motion, dusted in snow. When her phone vibrated, she smiled, sensing it might be Nic even before checking.

She read his message once... then again. *Something is changing him. He always had that gentleness and a thoughtful streak, but now he is becoming poetic also...*

Her fingers lingered over the screen, and then, she began to type, slowly, choosing each word with care.

Julia:

Your message felt like a feather landing in my evening.

The river dream still stays with me.

Maybe silence is the language of the soul...

Julia (continued):

Yes, let's walk soon. Let's go somewhere the city can't reach.

Somewhere we can hear the hush between the heartbeats of time.

She paused, then added, almost playfully:

Julia:
P.S. You're not the only one learning to listen.
The whisper is getting louder.

She hit send and placed the phone back on the windowsill.

CHAPTER 35

Winter Conversations

Snow had begun to fall again in Hyde Park, covering the pine trees and rooftops with a soft white hush. Julia and Nic had come to spend two weeks for Christmas and New Year here. And as usual they would mostly each stay at their parent's home but also just see how they would feel.

The world outside Julia's childhood home was still, as if holding its breath in reverence for the peace of the season. Inside, the scent of cinnamon and cloves drifted from the kitchen, mingling with the low sound of Mahalia Jackson's Christmas songs playing in the background.

Julia sat curled in the corner of the sofa, wrapped in one of her father's old flannel blankets. Nicolas sat next to her, a mug of hot chocolate between his hands. They had just come in from a long walk, cheeks flushed, scarves damp with melted snow.

Her mother, Elena, bustled in with a tray of butter cookies, still warm. She placed them down on the coffee table, dusted her hands on her apron, and gave them both a pointed look.

"Well," she said, with a dramatic little sigh, "you two look very cozy."

Julia smiled, already sensing the direction of the conversation.

Elena sat across from them, her eyes bright. "You've been together so long, childhood sweethearts, practically married already. When are you two going to give me something to really celebrate? A wedding? Maybe a little one around next Christmas?"

Nicolas choked softly on his hot chocolate. Julia let out a gentle laugh, half amused, half mortified. "Mom…"

"I'm just saying," her mother went on, undeterred. "You're both in your thirties. You're settled, you love each other. What's the hold-up? What are we waiting for?"

Before Julia could speak, her father's voice floated in from the dining area. "Elena, let them breathe. It's Christmas."

Elena raised her eyebrows but leaned back slightly. "I'm not pressuring. I'm just… nudging. With love."

There was a pause. Nicolas set down his cup and glanced at Julia. She met his gaze. It was a soft, knowing look, one that held no fear, but a quiet understanding that their path was unfolding at its own pace.

Julia spoke first. "We're really happy, Mom. We're… exploring life in a different way right now. I don't quite have words for it yet, but it's beautiful."

Her mother blinked, confused. "Exploring life in a different way? Like what?"

Julia hesitated. "Meditation. Silence. Spirituality. I've been learning to listen more... to life itself. I don't feel rushed. I just want to be, for a while."

Nicolas nodded. "It's true. I've been thinking a lot about my grandmother lately. The things she used to say when we hiked together. About the land, the stars, the soul. I think I'm starting to understand them. Maybe for the first time."

Elena looked between them, brows drawn. "But don't you want a family?"

"We have a family," Nicolas said gently, gesturing to her and to Julia's father. "Right now, we're both exploring our careers, yes, but we're also discovering something... deeper. About who we are and why we're here. The world can be a confusing place. And to be honest, I'm not sure I'd want to bring a child into it, not as we are now, and not as the world is now."

Julia nodded. "I think about that too. What are we bringing a child into? All the influences children are surrounded by today... social media, endless noise, overstimulation, pressures at such a young age. It feels like the world is raising them more than their parents."

She paused, watching her mother's expression change

"I'm still figuring out what life really is. And that journey needs space. Stillness. A kind of simplicity. Not the added responsibility of a child, not just yet, if we have a choice. And we do."

"There's also the stress and despair," Nicolas added quietly. "The peacelessness. So many children are raised by screens and systems. So much anxiety, disconnection. And I think, if I'm not even sure yet how to live with peace and balance, how can I teach that to someone else?"

Julia nodded again. "We're not saying never. But we want to be conscious. Not just follow a path because it's the next box to check. And honestly, I think the world needs more awakened adults, not just more children."

Her mother opened her mouth, then closed it again.

Nicolas continued. "We have so many hospitals, nurses, doctors, and medications. But people are more and more sick, physically, emotionally and mentally. And I'm asking myself… is something wrong with the system itself? With how we live? I admire how Julia has shifted toward a more plant-based nutrition. She's becoming gentler, more thoughtful. And I find myself wanting that too. Wanting to rethink what it means to live with dignity."

There was a quietness in the room now. The fire crackled. Outside, the snow continued to fall.

Elena stood up and walked to the window, arms crossed, watching the flakes dance through the light. "I just want you to be happy. And I worry sometimes… that maybe you'll wait too long and miss it."

Julia rose, walked over, and slipped an arm around her mother's waist. "We're not missing it. We're right in the middle of it."

Her mother turned, and for a moment, the strong, practical woman showed the soft glisten of unshed tears. "I know. I just… I love you both so much. And I want to see you rooted. Safe."

"We are," Julia whispered. "More than ever before."

In the quiet that followed, her father appeared at the doorframe, holding three plates with apple pie. "Peace offering," he said with a wink. "I've been experimenting with a version that's egg-free. The vegetarian edition. Shall we try?"

They all laughed.

And as they sat down together once more, spooning the apple pie into their mouths, they also savored the warmth of each other's company.

CHAPTER 36

On Intimacy

That night, the house had gone still. Julia's parents were asleep, their muffled voices having faded behind closed doors. Outside, the snow had turned the backyard into a moonlit wonderland, soft and glowing.

Julia sat cross-legged on her childhood bed, a warm shawl around her shoulders. Nicolas was stretched out beside her, leaning back on one elbow.

Neither of them spoke for a while. The silence between them wasn't awkward, it had never been. It was like a soft field they could both lie down in and just be.

Nicolas felt himself drifting inward. He was thinking about the conversation with Julia's mom. He remembered the meditations with Julia. He reflected on the soul, on innocence, on a golden time when life itself was dignified and harmonious.

And suddenly, he saw her.

His grandmother, sitting cross-legged on the forest floor, chin lifted slightly, eyes half closed, listening, not to him, but to the trees. To the earth. To something unseen. She would invite him to "play," but it wasn't the kind of play his classmates talked about. It was a quiet training, only now did he understand what it had been.

"Walk to the edge of the lake," she'd say, "and then come back. And listen to every birdcall. Tell me which ones were nearby and which were far."

Or, "Pick up three things with your eyes closed. Feel them. Smell them. Now tell me where they came from."

Sometimes she'd wake him before dawn, wrap him in a blanket, and walk with him barefoot through the dew until the sun rose, urging him to notice how the earth changed in the dark.

He remembered laughing, complaining, trying to keep up, but never questioning.

His grandmother had wanted to teach him everything her elders had taught her. The traditions, the ways of strengthening the body and sharpening the senses, not for sport, but for resilience.

But there were limits. His parents, loving but cautious, hadn't let her push too far. No fasting, no barefoot hikes in the cold. "We're not living on the reservation or in the wild anymore," his father had said once. "Let the boy be a boy."

Still, she had insisted on the Boy Scouts. It was the closest she could get him to the forest without raising eyebrows. And he'd gone, year after year, learning to tie knots and pitch tents, to start fires without matches and sit through storms without fear. But it was his grandmother who had taught him how to listen, to the wind, to his heartbeat, to the silence between thoughts.

He smiled faintly, realizing that what she had given him was more than just childhood memories, it was heritage. It was strength dressed in gentleness.

Julia turned toward him, eyes soft. "You okay?"

Nicolas smiled faintly. "Yeah. Just thinking about Grandma, and about your mom."

Julia rolled her eyes. "She means well. But you'd think she was auditioning for a grandmother-of-the-year competition." They both laughed softly, but the laughter faded quickly into something quieter.

"She's not wrong, though," Julia added gently. "I mean... we are a bit unconventional."

There was a pause between them.

"I don't know if I've told you," she said slowly, "but... I'm really okay with the way things are between us. I mean... the fact that we're not, you know... so physically intimate."

Nicolas nodded, deeply grateful she said it aloud. "Yeah," he said. "I've thought about it too. A lot, actually. But if I am really honest, I am okay with it too."

There was no shame or guilt between them, just clarity.

"I sometimes do feel the pressure," he continued, voice quiet. "The way guys talk at work, especially the younger ones, it's like everyone's trying to prove something. How wild their weekends are. Talk about hookups or passionate interactions with partners. And some even boast about the number of notches on their belt. Like... that's what makes them men." He shook his head. "I sit there, nodding, laughing maybe, but I don't relate. And more often than not it leaves me feeling kind of… sad. Or even a little disgusted. Like something beautiful is being thrown away for bragging rights."

Julia looked at him, moved by the honesty in his words.

"I used to wonder if something was wrong with me," he said. "But now… I think there's just something different about the space we've always given each other."

"When we were in our teens and twenties it was exciting, and we were curious. And there was the belief that love and a good relationship is defined by physical attraction, romance, passion, and sex. But we've been together for more than 15 years now. It feels more like… companionship. Safe. Real. Like I could just be. Like we didn't have to pretend to be what we weren't feeling."

She smiled. "Like close and best friends, in a way."

He chuckled. "Protective, but free."

The silence that followed was luminous.

Julia said quietly. "Familiar. Respectful and empowering. Not… wild, not stormy. Just soft."

He looked at her nodding in agreement.

There was a long pause.

Julia shifted, drawing the shawl tighter. "It's strange maybe. I don't miss… that kind of physical intimacy. I feel we're very connected and the friendship continues to grow. Isn't that love?"

Nicolas leaned forward slightly. "Yeah. Same. I never needed sex to feel close. And romance, passion and sex is so consuming, and frankly also exhausting. Also mentally and emotionally. Honestly, I feel more dignity and peace without it. Like nothing's missing."

Julia smiled, a soft light flickering in her eyes. "I've been thinking lately… maybe what we have is more about soul connection."

"You remind me again of Grandma," he said quietly. "She used to say love isn't always fire, it can be a still lake too. Clear. Reflective. Timeless. She used to say that a man's wisdom and strength gets blocked when his mind is entangled in pleasures of the body. That I should always be true, faithful and dedicated, but never make a show of my emotions. That I should know that sex and emotional dependency have nothing to do with love."

There was a stillness then. A quiet joy. Neither of them moved to touch, or kiss, or even hold hands.

After a while, Nicolas lay back fully and sighed. "Whatever we are and whatever we are becoming, Jules… I'm okay with it."

"Me too," she said.

CHAPTER 37

At the Van Wyck Table

The next evening found them at the Van Wyck home, a low-slung house with a wide porch and cedar trim, tucked beneath tall maples that now wore a blanket of snow. Inside, the soft glow of pendant lights bathed the dinner table in orange-golden warmth. Nic's mother, Caroline, had made roasted squash, cornbread, and a hearty cranberry-walnut salad. His father, James, had opened a bottle of wine and was serving roasted root vegetables with practiced ease. Because of Julia, they had decided to have a vegetarian dinner.

The four of them sat around the table in the easy comfort of old familiarity.

"So," Caroline said, passing the cornbread to Julia. "How's your mom doing?"

Julia laughed. "Busy as always. Between her thriving real estate business, church, and preparing for Christmas and New Year."

"And the two of you?" Caroline asked, her gaze warm. "How's the holiday so far?"

Nicolas and Julia exchanged a glance.

"Well…" Nicolas began, smiling, "last night was… interesting."

Julia chuckled. "My mom gave us an inquisition about marriage and babies."

Caroline raised her brows. "Ah."

James smiled knowingly and poured more sparkling water into Julia's glass.

"We talked a lot," Nicolas continued. "About how we're not really feeling called to that kind of life. At least not right now."

His mother gave a small nod. "I see."

"And it made me think of Grandma," he added, softer now. "I'm starting to understand her more."

Caroline looked up, and a deep silence crossed her face. "Really?"

"She used to talk about listening to the earth. About silence and stars. About walking gently. Back then I thought it was just myths and poetry. Now I think… it was wisdom. And I was too young to get it."

Caroline's eyes shimmered. "She would have loved to hear you say that."

"She was so different," Nicolas said, now leaning forward. "She always moved slowly, like nothing ever rushed her. But she was so strong. There was this calm in her. I feel like I've been chasing that ever since."

Caroline smiled, her voice low. "It's in you, Nic. That steadiness. That listening nature."

James glanced up from his plate. "You always had that contemplative streak. Even when you were five, you'd stare at trees for a long time like you were waiting for them to speak."

They laughed.

"I wanted to ask," Nicolas said, turning to his mother. "Can you tell some more about her? About her customs? The way your family lived before moving here?"

Caroline set down her fork, her eyes lighting with the quiet reverence of memory.

"Well," she said, "it was simple. Deeply respectful of nature. Everyone had a role, not one that was assigned, but one that fit you. The elders weren't just respected, they were consulted. Health wasn't just the absence of illness, it was self-control and balance. With yourself, with your food, your sleep, the land, the seasons. People knew how to fast, how to listen to their dreams, how to prepare medicines from the woods. But most of all, they knew how to observe. That was their greatest strength."

Nicolas was quiet, absorbing.

"Even the games they played as children," Caroline added, "were meant to sharpen the senses and to make the body strong. Walking in silence. Tracking without disturbing. Listening for a squirrel from fifty feet away. She used to say that to be alive was to be aware.

Grandma believed that this way of upbringing produced resilient, righteous adults who contribute positively to society. That children should cultivate sharp senses, physical strength and endurance, emotional resilience and moral character that would show truthfulness, generosity, and will-power.

She paused, as if thinking about how different life is now. She thought about the children at her school.

"The way she was brought up was not through lectures or punishment, but through games, observing the example of the adults and elders, stories, and small challenges woven into daily life."

Nicolas smiled "She used to tell me to listen with my whole body, not just with the ears. That I should not just eat anything, anytime, anywhere, but should be balanced. That the body serves the spirit, not the other way around."

"Yes." Caroline smiled, remembering her mother. "She used to have fixed times to eat and would never eat if not hungry.

She would insist on teaching you to hear subtle sounds, like the difference in a bird's call or the faint cracking of a twig in the woods. That this was not for hunting but would teach you determination, adaptability, patience, and inner stillness."

Julia listened, entranced.

After some time Caroline turned to her, curious. "Tell us about your meditation. Nicolas said that you have become serious about it."

Julia hesitated, then spoke slowly. "It slowly turned into... a kind of inner journey. I'm learning to experience myself as a spiritual being, a soul, not just a human personality, or a body with a schedule. A being of light, if that makes sense."

Caroline nodded, intrigued.

"And I've started to ask myself deeper questions," Julia continued. "Why am I here? Where was I before I was born? What is the source of love that doesn't fade? These questions... they don't scare me anymore."

There was a gentle stillness at the table.

James leaned back. "Sounds like the kind of questions people used to ask before we got too busy consuming and producing."

Caroline smiled at her husband, then turned back to Julia. "It does sound familiar. My mother believed we carry memories of a more harmonious world. A world we come from. And that silence helps us remember it."

Julia's eyes widened. "That's what I feel. Meditation helps me to remember."

Nicolas looked between the two women and smiled.

They were quiet again.

The snow had started falling again outside, brushing the windows with lace. The room glowed gently, and the warmth between them lingered like a low-burning but steady fire.

CHAPTER 38

Caroline and Julia

Later that evening, the house had softened into the quiet of firelight and slow conversation. The snow still fell gently, blanketing the yard in a fresh layer of stillness. Nicolas and James were cleaning up in the kitchen, trading stories from the hospital and the skies.

Caroline slipped on her coat, reached for her boots, then turned to Julia. "Want to take a walk? Just down to the pines and back."

Julia nodded, rising at once. "I'd love to."

The cold met them like a soft hush. They walked slowly, their boots crunching over fresh snow, breath mingling in pale clouds. The moon was low, veiled slightly by snow light, casting the trees in a bluish glow. It was peaceful in a breathtaking way.

Caroline was the first to speak. "You know, I liked what you shared at the table earlier. About returning to the essence of who you are."

Julia glanced over, touched. "Thank you."

"I've seen that kind of introspection before," Caroline continued. "My mom, when she fasted or went into silence, something would shift. She wouldn't speak for a day or two, but when she came out of it... there was power in her. Like she had touched something most people never find."

Julia nodded slowly. "That's how I feel in the mornings now. When I sit in that quiet... I feel connected to something pure. Constant. It helps me face the rest of the day without getting lost."

Caroline smiled faintly, but her eyes held something deeper. "I can see how strong that connection is becoming for you. But may I ask... where is it all going? I mean, how does this... fit with Nicolas?"

Julia took a breath, steady and open. "I'm not sure, but I feel that Nic and I are closer now then ever before and we understand each other better. But we are also letting each other free to explore what is important for each one.."

"I'm sure," Caroline said, her tone warm but clear. "I'm not here to push. It's just... as a mother, you wonder. Nicolas is very private, but I know when something's changing inside him. I see how much your journey has inspired him. I'm proud of that. And I also wonder what happens when two people change... in different directions."

Julia stopped walking for a moment and looked out over the moonlit yard, toward the dark line of trees at the edge of the land. Then she turned toward Caroline.

"I love him. That hasn't changed. And I don't feel we're growing apart,... only inward. Both of us. In our own ways."

Caroline studied her quietly.

Julia continued, voice soft but unwavering. "I know the next step for most couples is to start a family. It's tradition and seen as the natural rhythm of life. But I also feel, deeply, that the world we're in now needs something more than tradition. It needs inner strength. Wisdom. Awareness. It needs a return to integrity. I can't imagine bringing a child into the world just because it's the expected next chapter."

Caroline's brow furrowed, not out of disagreement, but reflection.

Julia went on, "What I'm practicing now, soul-consciousness, detachment, simplicity, celibacy, it's helping me re-think everything I thought life was about. I'm not closing the door to family. But I am questioning what it means to live with purpose. If I'm not centered first, what can I truly offer to anyone else?"

Caroline nodded slowly. "It's thoughtful. And brave."

Then, more gently, "But family is also about continuity. Belonging. That was always the teaching I grew up with, that we don't rush, but we do eventually plant. We continue the story. We pass it on."

Julia's voice softened, reverent. "I hear that. And I respect it deeply. Especially knowing where it comes from. Your way is full of wisdom."

They walked in silence for a few steps more.

Then Julia added, almost in a whisper, "But I'm starting to believe there are other ways to pass something on. Not through children, necessarily, but through how we live. Through those we touch during our life. Through the light we carry into every interaction. And as spiritual beings we never die."

Caroline looked at her for a long moment, the snow gently catching in her dark hair. Then she gave a slow, thoughtful nod. "That's something my mother might've said."

Julia smiled, heart full. "Maybe we're not so far apart after all."

"No," Caroline said. "Not far."

They turned to head back, the porch lights glowing warmly ahead, yellow-golden against the blue snow.

Before they reached the steps, Caroline touched Julia's arm. "Thank you for being honest. And for being with my son without trying to pin him down or expecting him to be how you are. That kind of love… it has its own power."

Julia swallowed, moved.

Caroline looked up at the stars, then back at her. "You've helped him return to what's always been in him."

They walked the rest of the way in silence, not needing to say anything more. The snow crunched gently underfoot. The pines were still.

And in the quiet, something unspoken passed between them. Respect. And perhaps, something deeper. Understanding.

CHAPTER 39

Love
Beyond Desires

The night had settled deep and still over Hyde Park. From Nicolas's old bedroom window, the world looked silver and asleep, tree branches rimmed in frost, the quiet glow of snow reflecting off the driveway. Somewhere in the distance, a dog barked once and then fell silent.

Julia lay on her side in bed under a thick quilt, facing Nicolas who was sitting on this old couch next to the bed, tucked under his very old favorite quilt that was made a long time ago by his grandmother. A single lamp cast a warm circle between them.

Neither spoke for a long while. It was a content silence, full like a field after rain.

Finally, Nicolas exhaled. "That was... a lot."

Julia smiled faintly. "Yeah. But in a good way."

He slid sideways on the couch and turned on his back, one arm tucked under his head, staring up at the ceiling. "I didn't think talking about Grandma would hit me like that."

"It was beautiful," Julia said, almost whispering. "The way your mom shared. The way you remembered her. It felt like... something ancient came alive in the living room."

Nicolas turned his head toward her. "I didn't realize how much I'd missed that part of me. Or how far I'd drifted from it. Medicine is all stats, files and scans. But with her, it was about watching the sky. Seeing what can't be measured."

Julia nodded. "I think I felt that too, tonight. A sense that real knowledge... doesn't shout. It whispers. And waits for us to be quiet enough to hear it."

He was quiet for a moment. "She used to say that in silence she returns to spirit."

Julia's eyes softened. "Maybe that's what we're both doing. Returning."

A pause.

"Maybe we were brought together," she said softly, "to journey together as souls. Not for marriage or children."

Nicolas looked at her for a long time. "You're not disappointed?"

"No, not really," she said, and meant it. "Are you?"

He shook his head. "Not anymore."

The room was warm, and the air had the cleanliness and freshness of a small town winter night. Something was shifting, not between them, but within them. A loosening of roles. A re-defining of love.

"I'm grateful," Julia said. "That we get to ask these questions. That we are open and honest about it. That we're not pretending."

Nicolas gave a tired smile without suppressing his relief. "Yeah. No pretending."

Another silence fell between them, so soft, so complete.

Outside, the wind moved gently through the trees. Inside, they lay quietly awake, not tangled in desire or plans, but wrapped in something far more enduring: truth, tenderness, and a shared threshold between who they were and who they were becoming.

CHAPTER 40

In Her Own Light

The room was quiet now. Nicolas had fallen asleep on the couch, his breathing deep and beneath the quilt, one arm resting over his chest. The soft rhythm of his rest added to the peace in the room.

Julia lay on the bed for a while, eyes open, watching the slow dance of shadows on the ceiling. Her thoughts weren't restless, but they were alive, gently stirring like leaves in an unseen breeze.

She slid out from under the covers, wrapped a shawl around her shoulders, and padded softly to the desk near the window. She switched on the small reading lamp, its circle of light like a quiet invitation,... and opened her journal.

For a moment she just sat there, listening to the silence.

Then, she began to write.

Something is changing. Not between us, but inside me.
I feel like I'm walking through a door I didn't know existed.
Not into a new life, but into a truer one.

And Nic... he's not blocking the way. He's holding his own space.
Not with demands, not with expectation. Just quietly.
It's so beautiful, such a kind form of love.
She paused. The pen hovered for a moment.
I don't know where this path leads.
But tonight, with his mother's stories, and the words that came from my own heart...
I felt something deep moving. A kind of remembering.
A time when people walked slower.
Looked inward.
Listened to the stars.

She gently closed the journal.

The snow was still falling outside, soft against the dark window. She stood and moved toward the little woven rug in the corner of the room. It wasn't her usual space, but it would do. She sat on the rug, spine upright, hands resting gently in her lap.

She let the outside world dissolve.

At first, all she did was observe her breath. The cool air entering. The warm air leaving. The body, steady and quiet.

Then came the feeling, familiar now, of shifting attention. Of detaching. Going beyond clutter and noise. Into silence. Into truth.

She saw herself, light, timeless, still. Not Julia the daughter, or girlfriend, or banker. Just... a being of light, light a tiny sparkling star. Whole and radiant. A traveler through time and space.

Deeply experiencing the self to be light, she sensed the nearness of another. An infinitely loving silent One. Gentle, pure. The Source of peace. The Supreme Soul.

Only light filled her mind. A deep sense of belonging and a quiet joy.

Stillness folded around her like a warm shawl. She sat in that state, not measuring time, not reaching for insight, just resting in the deep quiet.

The lamp still glowed. The snow still fell.

When she finally got up she reached over to her diary again and wrote:

I used to think that love needed to be proven through closeness, through touch, through passion, through claiming. But now I understand: the deepest kind of love doesn't grasp, does not take. It gives, empowers, and allows the greatness and beauty of the other to shine.

The past few years of the relationship with Nic have been increasingly defined not by passion, but more by friendship, not by wild or intense emotions, but by long conversations and refined feelings, by exploring what is important for us, by a certain purity.

Celibacy wasn't something we planned. But sex was not a rule nor an expectation or demand. And celibacy was not a rejection. It simply became what felt most natural for us. As we began to listen to the quieter voices within.

There is a power in conserving what the world tells you to spend.

By choosing silence, we began to hear more.

By stepping back from physical desire, we began to touch something sacred,... within ourselves.

It's strange... how much freedom lives on the other side of simplicity.

It is not a path of denial, but of re-direction. Our energies, once scattered in old patterns, now flow toward higher consciousness and toward the Supreme.

What we've found is not an absence of love, but its deepest form: love that uplifts, that liberates, that remembers what we truly are.

Spiritual beings.

Travelers.

Light.

Chapter 41

The Dream
of Light

The soft gray of morning was beginning to emerge at the edge of the sky. Snow still blanketed the world outside, muffling the sounds of the waking day. The air was still, and everything seemed suspended in a hush.

Julia moved.

Her eyes opened slowly, as if returning from another world. The edges of the room were blurry at first, but the feeling that lingered inside her was crystalline.

She lay still for a moment, barely breathing, as the dream unspooled itself in her memory.

There had been no form. No face. Just... light.

Not like the sunlight through trees or the glow of a candle, but something more alive. Conscious. A divine Presence that shimmered with peace, pure, golden, gentle, and yet radiant with joy so complete it almost made her weep.

The loving vibes had filled her with an otherworldly calm. Like standing inside a sun that did not burn, but healed. The Divine didn't speak, but she heard everything.

And what she felt, more than anything, was freedom.

Weightless. No longer bound by the gravity of worry or identity. She was only a being of light, returning to the Source. The Light recognized her. Loved her. Knew her.

She had no words for it. But her heart had understood.

Tears slipped from the corners of her eyes, warm against her temples.

She turned slightly and saw Nicolas still sleeping on the couch, his breath slow and even, one hand curled gently near his chest. The peacefulness on his face mirrored the peace still echoing from her dream.

Julia sat up slowly and wrapped her shawl around her shoulders. The house was quiet. She crossed to the window and looked out.

The snow had stopped. The sky was now pale rose and pearl.

She placed a hand lightly on the glass.

God is real, she thought. Not distant, not a concept. But Someone alive. Someone near. A Being filled with a love so vast it cannot be imagined, only experienced.

And she had experienced it. Not in a temple. Not in a book.

But in the silence. In her mind. In surrender.

She closed her eyes, and the memory came rushing back, that beautiful, eternal One.

It was a kind of bliss that didn't come from anything in this world. Not from achievements or wealth, or sense pleasures or human approval. It was older than the world. It was before everything.

And it was hers.

Tears welled again, not from sadness, but from gratitude. From awe.

She pressed her palms together in front of her chest and bowed slightly toward the dawn-lit sky.

"Thank you," she whispered.

And as the first sunray kissed the snow outside, Julia stood still in the light, no longer searching, no longer needing proof. She had experienced the company of her spiritual Father, and He had awakened something within that could never go back to sleep.

Later that morning, after a shower and a cup of tea, Julia opened her journal again. The same journal she had written in the night before, now felt like a sanctuary.

She uncapped her pen and let the words come, slowly.

This morning I woke from a dream that wasn't really a dream.
It was more real than waking life.
There was no image, no form.
Only Light... alive, conscious, peaceful, joyful.

The Light didn't speak, but I heard everything.
The Light didn't move, but I felt embraced.
He wasn't human, and yet He knew me better than anyone
ever has.
God. As Light.
Not as judge. Not un-reachable. Not un-knowable.
But as a Friend, a loving Presence, in the dimension of light
and silence, beyond.
The moment I was near that Light, I remembered who I am,
not a role, not a body, not a mortal human.
Just a soul. A star.
Free. Loved. Eternal.

She paused, the pen resting softly against the page.

I don't want to lose this feeling.
This knowing.
So I'll keep returning to that silence.

She closed the journal gently, holding it for a moment against her chest.

Outside, the snow had begun to melt slightly in the rising sun. Drops slid down the windowpane like tiny offerings.

And deep within, Julia knew: something in her life had turned a page, not outwardly, but inwardly. Quietly, permanently.

She had met the One, she had met the Light.

And now, she would never forget the way Home.

Afterword

Celibacy is often misunderstood.

To the world, it may seem like absence, of passion, of intimacy, of connection.

For some, the word evokes austerity or distance.

But to those on a spiritual path, celibacy is not absence. It can become a doorway not into isolation but to emerging innate inner beauty.

It is the flowering of a deeper awareness of self not as a bodily being but as a spiritual being, a soul.

In the story you've just read, Julia and Nicolas never set out to live without romantic or physical closeness.

Rather, they followed something more delicate.

A longing for clarity, freedom, and truth.

As they each began to discover themselves something shifted.

Their bond remained, but the form of their love evolved.

Celibacy, in the spiritual sense, is not about suppression. It is about focusing on the invisible and the eternal, on the non-physical as the source of love, peace, and truth.

It is the conscious choice to conserve energy, to turn inward instead of outward, to experience higher consciousness rather than chase physical connection and short-lived pleasures.

Across traditions, whether called brahmacharya in Indian and Buddhist philosophies, consecration in monastic Christianity, or simply, 'choosing solitude', this path has long been honored for its transformative power.

Benefits often spoken of include:

Clarity of mind, inner stability, freedom from emotional entanglement. A deeper experience of the self and the Divine, dignity and self-respect.

But beyond benefits, celibacy, when chosen with awareness, can become an act of love. Love for the self, the soul. Love for the Supreme Soul. Love that seeks not to possess or perform, but to uplift, to bless, and to simply be.

As Julia wrote:

"The more I remember that I'm a soul, a being of light, the less I feel the pull of outward seeking. There's something empowering in connecting to our virtuous nature of benevolence and giving. It lets me love, care, and appreciate. Truly. Without clinging. Without needing.

"The awake self doesn't crave touch, but radiates light. And when I'm in a soul-aware state, I don't need love. I become love."

And as Nicolas reflected:

"Celibacy, I realize, is not emptiness. It's concentration. It's the quiet power of not leaking energy into desires that don't match the soul's natural nature. I want my love to uplift, not entangle. To honor, not bind.

"The more I let go of the physical identity, the more I find clarity. Celibacy has made space in me, not just for peace, but for truth. It's not the suppressing or absence of desire, it's the presence of something higher."

In the end, their journeys were not about leaving something behind, but about stepping into something higher. Celibacy was not the destination. It was the sign that they were remembering who they truly were.

Not a woman.
Not a man.
But a soul.
A point of living light.

Free. Aware. Complete.

About Meditation

The Brahma Kumaris World Spiritual Organization offers a gentle, accessible form of meditation called Raja Yoga, which invites you to explore the soul, the dynamics of the mind, and your connection with the Supreme.
It's simple, open to everyone, and always free of charge.

Whether you are new to meditation or looking to deepen your practice, you're warmly invited to visit one of our Meditation Centers.

Visit manhattanmeditationcenter.org to get informed of the activities in Manhattan, New York.

Visit brahmakumaris.us to explore free courses, guided meditations, and centers in the USA.

Visit brahmakumaris.org for international locations.

About the Author

Rona's journey began in the Netherlands, where she was born to parents of mixed European Indonesian heritage, while she grew up in multi-cultural and multi-religious Surinam, South America.

Her spiritual path with the Brahma Kumaris started in 1991, driven by a curiosity about the dynamics of the human mind and a heartfelt desire to serve humanity. With a background in medicine, Rona gained hands-on experience in general medicine, psychiatry, and geriatrics in the Netherlands. However, for over 18 years now, she has dedicated herself fully to the work of the Brahma Kumaris, leaving her medical practice behind.

Rona has helped to establish Brahma Kumaris Meditation Centers across the Dutch Caribbean, the Dominican Republic, Haiti, and Puerto Rico. At present, Manhattan, New York, is her base.

She is also the author of the book "Experience Meditation", sharing insights and practical guidance on Raja Yoga meditation.